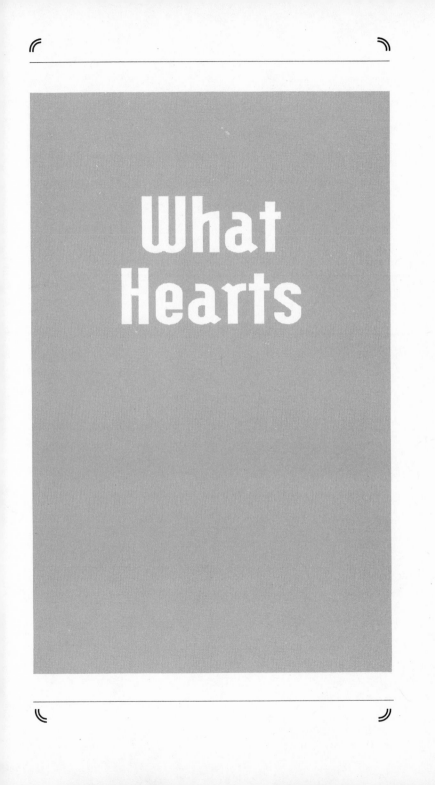

What
Hearts

Bruce Brooks

What Hearts

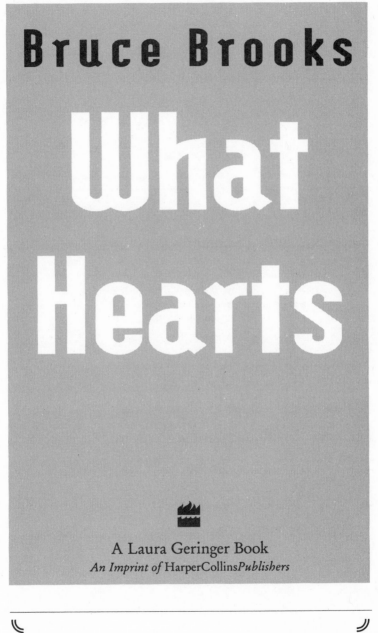

A Laura Geringer Book
An Imprint of HarperCollins*Publishers*

The author, gratefully acknowledges the use
of excerpts from the following poems:
"Little Boy Blue" by Eugene Field, from *Poems of Childhood*,
originally published by Charles Scribner's Sons.
"The Highwayman" by Alfred Noyes, from *Collected Poems*,
originally published by J. B. Lippincott.

WHAT HEARTS

Library of Congress Cataloging-in-Publication Data
Brooks, Bruce.
    What hearts / by Bruce Brooks.
        p.   cm.
    "A Laura Geringer book."
    Summary: After his mother divorces his father and remarries, Asa's
sharp intellect and capacity for forgiveness help him deal with the
instabilities of his new world.
    ISBN 0-06-021131-8. — ISBN 0-06-021132-6 (lib. bdg.)
    [1. Remarriage—Fiction.   2. Stepfathers—Fiction.]   I. Title.
PZ7.B7913Wh 1992   92-5305
[Fic]—dc20   CIP
                                                                 AC

Typography by David Saylor
2 3 4 5 6 7 8 9 10

Contents

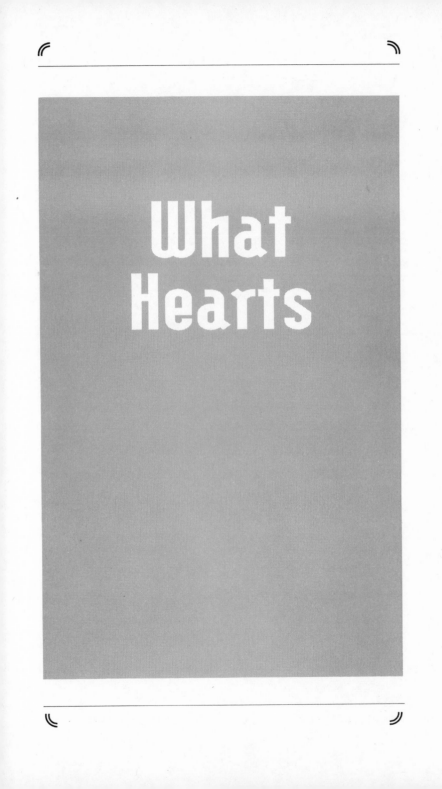

What
Hearts

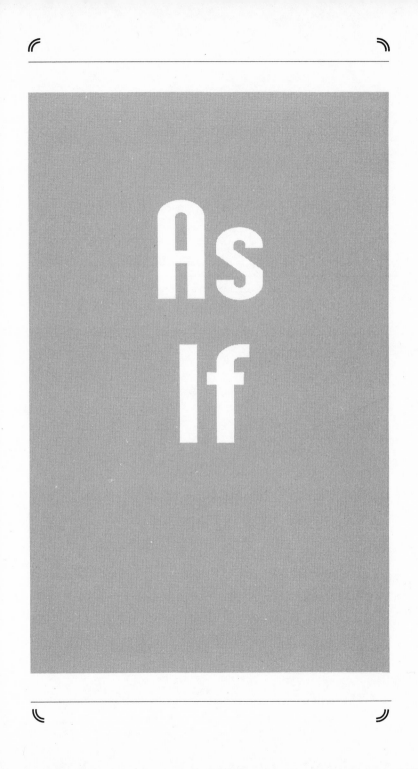

As
If

O N E

ASA WAS AMAZED THAT HE LEFT FIRST GRADE WITH SO
much stuff. As he ran down the winding tar path
that led through the woods to the street, he took a
quick inventory: his knapsack, straining at its
straps, held a blank blue composition book and
three unsharpened yellow pencils (for a summer
journal; everyone had gotten these), a battered
hardback copy of a book called *The Little Prince*
(no one else had received this; the librarian had
slipped it in secret to "my best little reader"), a
mimeographed copy of the school handbook complete with all kinds of forms to be brought in on
the first day of second grade in September (everyone, of course), six certificates stamped with foil
medallions (one for completing the dumb first-
grade reader with its "See Spot jump!" stories, one
for being able to print the alphabet in upper and

lower case, one for being able to sing "The Star-Spangled Banner" and "You're a Grand Old Flag," all of which everyone got, even Gordon Firestone, who never got the words right to the latter song and still couldn't tell the difference between small "d" and "b," "g" and "q"; the other three were from gym class, for being able to run and jump and roll (some boys had gotten more than the three, but they were show-offs); a big, glossy black-and-white photograph of the whole class (for everyone, even the two kids who had missed school on the day the picture was taken; Asa had been sick with a bad cold himself, but his parents had made him come for the picture, in which he was the only child wearing a jacket and tie); and, finally, a report card. Everyone had gotten a report card too, even Ronnie Wells, though the word was that he would have to repeat the year. Everyone had gotten one, a sky-blue cardboard report card with six boxes on it for final grades written in heavy black ink, grades for the whole year, grades summing up everything the kid had done; *everything*—but only Asa's card held an *A* in each box, sharply drawn, lined up like six pointed missiles blasting off into a perfect future. Perfect! He was perfect, and he was the only one. Subtly, under the guise of friendly interest, he had checked: he had seen everyone else's card except Ronnie's (poor Ronnie could be fairly disregarded), and they all had at least one *B*. Rita Pennington had been closest; only her crinkly left-handed handwriting had kept her from sharing the pinnacle with Asa. He had a crush on Rita, but he was glad she had gotten a *B* in Penmanship. This made him ashamed, but there it was. Besides, she had won the lottery for the class hamster, so no one should feel too sorry for her.

In addition to the treasures in his pack Asa clutched one more in his right hand: a bunch of fresh, hand-planted, hand-watered, hand-weeded, hand-picked radishes. He looked at them quickly; they were not believable. Nothing could become that color underground. Such a red had to be made by craft; surely it would take scientists, geniuses, to design the proper chemical sequence! Asa had chosen to plant radishes in the class garden when the first graders had pored over seed packets in February, simply because he did not believe they would come true. Today, just this morning, everyone had been allowed to undo all the work that had gone into keeping the vegetables hidden in the ground: they ripped their things out, shook the brown clods off them, and almost cried with revelation. Really: everyone, not just Asa, almost cried. The long orange carrots had been a hit, but the radishes stole the show. No one else had wanted to plant them, because they had all been thinking about *eating* what they grew. Asa had been thinking about *growing* what he grew, as an end in itself. But tonight he and his dad and his mom would all eat this wonderful redness. He was triumphant.

As he approached the crosswalk, he worked one of his thirty-one radishes free from the tangle of greens and knobs, so that he could give it to Nadine, the policewoman whom he had seen twice a day through kindergarten and first grade, who had given him his first nickname ("Well hey, Ace—how you this morning?"), who allowed him his first joke of pretend mockery ("Fine, Captain— you caught any criminals yet?"). He stepped into the crosswalk.

Before Nadine could greet him, he held out a

radish to her. She drew her chin back to focus on it and shook her head. "No, I don't love a radish. Thank you all the same, Ace." She looked beyond him, wheeling her arm at a slowpoke. Asa was perplexed by the idea of not loving a radish, but he went on as he walked, turning backward so he could face her: "I got straight *A*'s, Captain. For the *year*."

"You have a nice summer," she said, and went to help a kindergartner who was about to cry pick up a splaying fan of papers he had dropped. Asa hesitated, then turned back around toward home and kept walking.

Well, maybe Bobby Levy would be more interested in what Asa had to share. In two minutes he would pass beneath the balcony on which Bobby always perched, only two feet off the uphill-slanting sidewalk but high enough to look down from. Bobby's private school dismissed a half hour earlier than the public school, and Bobby spent that extra time watching TV. He made a point of waiting for Asa every afternoon with the blue-silver rectangle of a television set shining deep in the dark room behind him, implying pointedly the thirty minutes of fun Asa had missed by being so unwisely unprivate. During the thirty seconds in which Asa, walking resignedly uphill, was within the range of Bobby's voice, Bobby, glib as a squirrel, always managed to chatter out a snappy summary of the rerun of *I Love Lucy* or *The Real McCoys* just for him. The summaries were remarkably clear, and Asa silently admired them even as he reminded himself that he disliked television comedies.

In fact, Asa never spoke to Bobby at all. It was not part of the relationship. Bobby had something to say, and Asa was the listener; he received, and passed by. Once, in the fall, he had tried to turn the TV report into a conversation, but Bobby had glared at him, cranky and affronted; in the middle of Asa's second sentence he snapped "*Father Knows Best* is on *right now!*" and huffed through the sliding glass doors, pulling the curtains closed behind him. But today would be different. Asa had something to talk about, today. A radish, but more, too: those triangular black-ink *A*'s were poised tensely in his awareness like the heads of arrows on a bowstring, and he might have to let them fly.

He looked ahead. Bobby, perched alertly on his balcony, was ready with his clipped, slightly bored tone, to begin: "So, Fred and Ethel win a trip to Cuba in a contest, but they entered under Ricky's name because they thought it would help them . . . " or something like that. Asa's heartbeats got quick. He knew he had to time this just right. If he let Bobby start his monologue, he would never be able to break in. He watched Bobby's rabbity top teeth against his lower lip, and he walked, closer and closer. When he was within ten feet, the top teeth lifted. Asa shouted, "Bobby, I grew some radishes. And I got a book, about a prince, and I got straight *A*'s!" He came to a stop beneath the balcony, and motioned that he wanted to toss Bobby the radish Nadine had refused.

Bobby stared down at him. He made no move to receive the offered radish. At last, after lifting his teeth a couple of times, he frowned and said, "I'm afraid there will be no more afternoon TV for you in the fall. You see, I'm starting piano. I *am* sorry for you." Then he turned and went inside. This time he did not bother with the curtains.

Asa stood for a moment. He held up his right

hand and looked at the radishes. It was true that the greens were wilting pretty severely. But the red was fine. So were the grades in his knapsack; so was the prince in his book. He shrugged his shoulders in case Bobby was looking, and turned toward home. He knew his mother was there. She was waiting for him. But—just imagine!—she had no idea about all this that was coming. It was as if the marvels he held right here in his hand and knapsack were not already certain—but they were, they were. She was in for some surprises, she and his father—especially his father: *there* was a guy who would know how to appreciate a radish. Asa stepped up his pace for home, full of the generous superiority of knowing exactly what you were about to give.

TWO

His mother was wearing a coat. This he could see, as he turned the corner and glanced ahead down the narrow sidewalk that ran in front of the apartments. She was sitting on something on the small stoop, looking straight ahead into the patios of the apartments across the green. Why wasn't she looking in the direction she knew he would be coming from? Why was she wearing a coat? It was cool under the dense leaves of the high trees, but a coat was not right, not in Maryland in June. A coat was not right. As if to protest, Asa shivered. And as he closed in on her, he recognized the object she was sitting on. It was a large suitcase of black pebbled imitation leather. It looked new.

She heard him and turned her head. He met her eyes. She stood up, her hands squeezed together in front of her. He looked at the suitcase briefly, then watched as she stared down at it and moved a step away, as if she expected something to open it from within now, and climb out.

"Asa," she said, looking up. "I have something to tell you." She was shaking her hands up and down, clenched together. He would not have been surprised if she had suddenly opened them on a downstroke and dice had shot out and rolled onto the sidewalk. She often rolled off the board at games, because she threw too hard, as if serious effort would turn up better numbers.

"Asa," she said, "son." Her face was moving in pieces; as he watched, the mouth twisted with one hard emotion, the eyes bulged with another that was softer, and the forehead twitched away from all these feelings. "Listen," she said.

But he did not. He leaped nimbly past her onto the porch, pulled and pushed his way through the screen door and the wooden door, and then found himself in nobody's living room. That is how it hit him: when he had left for school that morning, the room had been his family's, full of sofas and rugs and tables that belonged to him—but now it was empty, and it was nobody's room. The sunlight slanted in through the windows across from him and made a weird shiny rhombus on the bare floor.

Behind him, through the screen door, he heard his mother still talking. He was not listening, but he heard her. As he stared around the room—floor as spiffy as a pond with new ice, walls that looked forcefully flat, as if they were pulling away from him in four directions at once—he assembled the fragments of sound that joined him in the room, and made them into a summary of the facts, reciting them to himself in a dull but clear voice that he barely recognized as his own: your mother and father do not love each other anymore. There is to be something called a divorce. It is for your sake. Your father is gone, and soon you will be, too.

He walked away from the voice and made a complete circuit of the empty place. Nobody was at home, throughout.

THREE

ON THE WAY TO THE AIRPORT IN THE TAXI, ASA ASKED no questions, yet his mother continued to talk. She had talked the whole time they waited on the stoop, until a taxi had come—called in advance, the boy realized, to arrive just ten minutes after his return from school. The taxi driver was from India, and the colors of his skin and hair would normally have fascinated Asa, but not now.

The man politely loaded the suitcase and knapsack into the taxi's trunk, then held the door for

Asa's mother. But instead of getting in, she stood straight, facing the man, and pulled Asa to stand beside her. With her arm around him, she smiled down, gave him a shake, then looked at the taxi driver and said, "This little boy's parents are getting a divorce. So we have to go to the airport and fly away to the beach." She smiled at the driver as if the next move were his. Asa watched as the man tried to acknowledge the cheer of her smile yet register an appropriately sober concern for her news. Somehow he managed to pull it off. Asa admired his dexterity.

His mother continued to stand and smile. Asa pulled away and got into the car.

As they drove through Washington Asa looked out at the city. This was his city, his and his father's; this had been their city. Perhaps it would continue to be his father's—he did not know. He knew that he and his mother were moving to her childhood home in North Carolina, after an overnight visit to a beach on the way. He had been to North Carolina on visits, and did not much like it. It was full of white people who seemed to him overconfident and overfriendly, and black people who seemed to fake those same qualities and then hide. He liked Washington.

"The whole world is in this town," his father used to tell him as they drove through the streets, pointing out the Venezuelan embassy or a Japanese grocery or a parade of Pakistanis holding banners. His father sold things to physicians and pharmacists. Once every couple of months he had to call on every doctor and druggist in town. He took Asa with him a lot in the years before school, and then during the summer following kindergarten. They drove around, saw things, discovered nifty little parks where they played a quick bit of catch or newsstands where they bought unusual comics. They went to the zoo or aquarium in between drugstores, they ate odd brown sandwiches in small restaurants where all the other customers were Middle Eastern or Portuguese. Not a downtown day went by in which he did not hear at least four languages spoken around him.

Now, in the taxi, his mother was speaking her own language, bringing him up to date with her ongoing explanation: He would see his father sometimes. His father still loved him. She still respected his father. She didn't love him, but she respected him. He was not a bad man.

Then Asa's mother said something that made him sit up and look at her sharply. She said someone was going to meet them at the beach. A man was going to meet them there. His name was Dave. She said Asa would like Dave very much.

Asa stared. His mother repeated her last sentence, about how he would like Dave very much. Then she stopped again, looking frightened by Asa's stare.

"You will like Dave," she tried a third time.

Asa said nothing. He stared her down. The cab made a left turn, then a right. The city bumped by. Finally, as they slipped over the banks of the Potomac onto the 14th Street bridge and left D. C. behind, Asa spoke. "Yes," he said, "maybe so. Maybe I will like him. But the question is—will I respect him?"

His mother said "Oh!" and slapped him across the mouth, and lunged across his lap in a heap, chuckling out sobs that seemed to come from someone he didn't know. He patted her hair as faintly as possible while her back heaved up and down. Heat came from her scalp. Asa looked up and met the pained eyes of the driver in the rearview mirror.

"It is all right, sir?" asked the driver.

"No," said the boy. "It is not all right at all."

FOUR

DAVE WAS NEARLY BALD. THIS SURPRISED ASA, AND right away he felt sorry for the man, as if thinning hair were a crippling strike of fate to be borne with bravery. The boy found himself feeling it was too easy to dislike someone who was bald, so he also found himself making a fabulous effort in the other direction, toward fondness. As they walked through the small airport and across a hot parking lot to Dave's old car, Asa gabbed straight to him with startling chipperness—about the flight, about Washington, about the taxi drive, and, in the greatest detail, about a school play that had ended the first grade in triumph that very afternoon, a play in which he had brilliantly played the lead part of The Prince—a play that in fact had not, as he was perfectly aware, taken place at all.

Dave seemed a little perplexed at the boy's zippy attack of goodwill; he pulled himself askance a bit, nodding or grunting without comment, unencouraging but mildly congenial. But Asa's mother watched her son with glowing beatitude, as if she had always known the two would get along just *fine*.

A couple of times, in the car, Dave had to interrupt Asa's chatter to say something about their destination. Whenever this happened, Asa, who was standing on the hump in the floor just behind the middle of the front seat, jounced up and down and resumed his narrative at the earliest verbal opening. In a way, he wasn't involved with this frantic speech; his intelligence seemed to be standing back, watching the show and wondering when it would stop. His mother, whose bliss had begun to lose its glow fast, held her hands to her temples, then brought them down sharply and turned on him. She remembered to smile, barely. Asa was in the middle of a description of his last season as the center fielder for a D. C. Little League team called the Jaguars, telling Dave with keen detail how he had caught a would-be last-inning grand-slam home run by toppling over the fence, then trotted dejectedly as if with an empty glove into the in-field as if the game were over—and then touched second and first with the ball revealed in his mitt, for the world's only unassisted triple play by an outfielder. Considering he did not even own a baseball glove, it was an excellent bit of story-telling.

"Honey," his mother said. Asa went into his jig-gling pause. "Honey, Dave is tired." She looked at Dave as if for confirmation.

But Dave grinned straight ahead and said, "Oh, I don't know. I'm feeling pretty fresh, actually. Love to hear if maybe the kid ever hit a big home run, or maybe starred in a movie. I bet he has. I bet he could remember if he thinks back. *Love* to hear that one." He grinned even harder, and flicked a glance at Asa's mother. Asa caught an edge of the glance. He was surprised to see that it was com-pletely, unmistakably, mean. In that instant all of Asa's energy swooped away from him, and he was left silent, calm and relieved. He was free to hate Dave now. He sat back.

Dave made a couple of comments to goad him into stretching out again, but Asa looked out the window. They were passing a beach. He stared at the ocean, and when a motel interposed itself between him and the ocean he tried to keep his eyes focused on the distance, so that when the ocean came back into view it would be clear. It was a strange game, and he could do it, but he couldn't figure out how he did it.

Dave scolded his mother for messing up a great friendship just when it was starting to get going. His mother said nothing. Dave laughed. He certainly laughed a lot. He did not seem to notice that he was bald.

By now it was early evening. There was no question about going to the beach; without ceremony or pretense, the three of them had dropped the idea that they had come here so that Asa could splash away his newfound sadness beneath the coppery sunshine, surrounded by sand castles and chortling kids eating bright Popsicles and the whole bit. It had been an idea, and Asa appreciated it as such. His mother was always kind in her ideas. When her plans never really made it off the paper into 3-D, Asa had learned to let the thought stand for something, and pass on.

Dave pulled up in front of a small square bungalow about the same size as his car. It was posing as a miniature house painted dark red, with a tiny window and shutters and a window box containing pink plastic geranium blossoms but no plastic greenery on the plastic stems. Asa thought perhaps birds had yanked the leaves off for use in their nest building; at home he had watched many songbird species binding their little baskets with leaves, and others using pieces of plastic bags or fishing line found in the trashy nooks people forgot about when they threw things away. Dave heaved his mother's suitcase and his knapsack out of the car's trunk, put them onto the macadam that went right up to the bungalow's front doorjamb, and handed his mother a key on a green plastic triangle.

She looked at it as if it were something utterly out of place here, a rubber tomahawk, perhaps, or a handful of snails. She appeared to be lost. "But where are you?"

Dave pointed to the next bungalow. "Number 10."

"Is ours 9, or 11?" asked Asa.

Dave shrugged. "Beats me. Lady just gave me my lucky number and the one next door. Ask her if you like." He leaned closer and pointed up the macadam drive, past other bungalows lined up like Monopoly houses. "You can find her in the bigger one at the end. She'd love to hear about you being a king and all, I'm sure. After that, you could tell her about the baseball."

"David," said Asa's mother.

"Just thought maybe the boy could chat for thirty or forty minutes while we got a basket of fried oysters," he said. "No harm." Then he went to his bungalow and opened the door without a key.

Asa and his mother stood there a minute. The light around them was turning quickly from orange to twilight blue. Some swallows cut through the air above the driveway like tiny scythes. Asa's mother sighed.

"David and I went to high school together," she said. "Back before your father and I met. He's known me a long time. He's *liked* me for a long time. Sometimes that makes him a little possessive." She smiled in Asa's direction; her teeth looked luminous in the blue dusk. "A girl likes that, sometimes." She held her smile, then took a step toward him and held out her hand. "I believe you understand, don't you?"

Asa plucked the key from the hand reaching out, and went for the door. "Of course not," he said.

FIVE

AFTER DINNER THE THREE OF THEM WALKED ALONG the boardwalk. To Asa, it was as if he had stepped inside a movie about some kind of carnival: he could smell the roasted popcorn and caramel and cotton candy and cigar smoke, he could hear the squeals of teenagers and the constant thunking of bare heels on the boardwalk; but somehow nothing touched him. He could see bellies protruding over Bermuda-shorts belt lines, with a carroty light seeping through pale Banlon shirts from the sunburned skin beneath, and thick faces full of laughter. But none of the whirling faces looked at him. He was just as glad. He was content just to walk, secure in the growing and marvelous conviction that nothing around him could break through.

But then Dave stopped and pointed off above their heads. "Now there's something for the boy," he said. "Come on." And he struck off in a new direction, leaving them to follow. Asa could not really see where they were heading, but as they left the main stream of the boardwalk behind them, he noticed a new noise. It was a ratchety rumble that came in surges, curving in and out of loudness. They were moving toward whatever was making it.

And then they were there. Set off from the boardwalk a bit was a small wooden pier, built on straight black pilings that disappeared into the tilting black water. Underneath, everything was very dark, and although he was up amid the noise, Asa could tell it was silent down there.

On top of the pier, there were six or ten or fifty

different rides, with big metal spheres and cabinets and cars spinning and jerking in space, all run by chugging machinery. People were being spun and jerked in the brightly painted cars and spheres; their eyes rolled, their hands waved, their throat muscles convulsed and their mouths stretched open as if to take bites of something just out of reach in the night air, but Asa could hear nothing from them. Only the machinery had a voice.

They entered the area by stepping through an arch made of pocked tin sheeting painted white, with a couple of hundred small round red light bulbs standing out along its outer edge like hair on end. "Here we go," said Dave. Now he stayed closer, even sliding an arm around Asa's shoulders and pulling him along. They wound between the veering armatures and cars of many rides, bearing out toward the end of the pier, where it grew darker, and much quieter. Finally, they arrived at a small platform where a man leaned against a rail, chewing on a piece of pencil as if it were a toothpick, his arms crossed, showing a purple tattoo on each that said FIGHT above a monochrome stars and stripes. There were steps. Dave pushed Asa up them.

"Got a boy here," said Dave, reaching into his back pocket and pulling out his wallet. The man did not say anything. Dave pulled out a bill and handed it to him. The man took it and dropped it into a cigar box from which the lid had been torn, sitting on a greasy flat surface among the cogged wheels and oily struts. Without turning toward Asa, he gave a small backhanded wave that Asa knew was meant for him: he had been admitted, he could ride.

But what was he to ride? He took a look. Up against the edge of the platform stood a train of four cars with thick leather seats inside. They were open on the top, and their sides were cut away in sweeping curves edged with nickel. They looked like the bodies of extremely heavy sleighs, without runners, without winter. Asa looked ahead of the front car. Two rails stretched a short distance, then banked sharply to the right and dipped out of sight. Beyond, where they would have gone had they not fallen away, was the ocean, looking like tar.

He turned back toward Dave and his mother

and the man. Dave smiled and gestured at the cars. "Go ahead," he said. "Have yourself a ball." He smiled and gestured, once, twice, three times. Asa did not get in. Dave looked at him straight, took a step toward him, and said in a softer voice, man to man: "Don't worry. Go on. It's just for you." He paused. "You *deserve* it."

Asa got in the third car. Immediately the tattooed man sprang up the steps. He leaned into Asa's car to lower a chrome bar in front of Asa's ribs, then he snap-locked a flimsy chain across the flashy curve of the side's cutaway.

He hopped off the platform and reached his hand into the darkness of the machinery. Asa saw something move, something upright, surprisingly tall, and his car moved forward six inches with a jolt as something latched onto it just below Asa's tailbone. The man had hold of a huge wooden lever, perhaps seven feet tall. It looked like a giant oar with its fat end wedged somewhere deep in the cogged wheels. The man held the lever solemnly, looked briefly at Asa, and pulled it, with a precise, decisive yank. Asa's car bolted forward.

He could not keep up with any sort of sequence

after that. He was flying at the ocean one second, then he was pinned beneath the chrome bar and a thousand pounds of air the next, then he was hurled upward and outward to the left, his thighs straining against the bar, then something as large as the ocean but invisible and dry was pulling him down and to the right, squeezing his face sideways into the leather and nickel. Nothing lasted for more than an instant, and nothing stopped.

It was too big and irresistible to be frightening; there was no point to being scared. Instead, he tried to see things. If he could see a few quick things, even in flickers, he could understand, and if he could understand, he could figure out what he could do and what he could not. He saw the ocean, tilted right, tilted left. He saw the car in front of him, always going in a different direction from the way he was moving. He saw the sky, and when he was thrown toward it he felt he was falling upward. Once, twice, three times he saw heads, arms, and clothes, and he assembled the flashes of them into his mother, Dave, and the tattooed man.

He wanted to see them more clearly, so he

worked at it. He found his body had roughly learned the sequence of thrusts and twists and drops, and he figured out which slingings preceded the glimpse of the three people. He began to prepare for the instant when he flashed by them, aligning his body with the movements so his head would stay upright, his vision level. Four, five, six times he whizzed by, seeing them longer each time. He was getting a decent look now—he could see three forms, he could see their heads turned toward him. It was okay.

But then on one whiz-by, the forms had changed. There were only two. On the next he saw they were Dave and the tattooed man. On the next he saw Dave gesturing, his hand hanging between the men, still as if in a photograph; on the next he saw only the tattooed man, putting something in his pocket.

Asa heard himself shriek. He could do it now, he could stay upright enough to keep the column of air open from his gut to his mouth, and he called up shriek after shriek and launched them into the air. He was not looking anywhere but up, and he realized that to someone far away he too would seem to be trying to bite something out of the sky, like the people whom he had been unable to hear. But he knew he was being heard. He kept it up.

And then it was over. The train of cars slowed; everything stopped. He was sitting in the seat, the bar against his ribs. His mouth was open but silent. His mother was grabbing at him from the platform. She grabbed him beneath the arms and tried to pull him out, but the bar kept him in; she was weeping and calling him as if he were not right there. He said nothing. He had not yet adjusted to being free of the grip of the big ride, or perhaps he would have told her, quietly, that it was all right, at least for now.

SIX

HE AND DAVE STOOD OUTSIDE A TELEPHONE BOOTH ON a silent street a few blocks inland from the boardwalk. His mother was inside the booth, speaking with his father. She looked a bit raw, and the light inside the booth seemed to fall sharply on her, like an astringent for skinned knees. The boy and the man said nothing as they watched her.

Asa held a string that led to a pale red balloon. It had been a lustrous ruby color when he had picked it out uninflated, but when the helium expanded it, the color faded. The balloon was a treat bought for him by Dave, but Dave had not especially wanted to give it. Asa's mother had insisted. Dave had gotten very angry at him for stopping the roller coaster. He had yelled at Asa, called him a sissy and other things, spun him around by the shoulders, and pushed him back into the roller coaster car, saying he would damn well get right back on the horse. Asa's mother had intervened, grabbing Dave by the shirt front and telling him a few things. Dave stomped off, first retrieving some money from the tattooed man. They followed, but his mother caught up to Dave and talked to him fiercely, matching him step for step. After a few minutes they bought the balloon.

Now his mother was talking to his father. Asa waited. There was nothing to say to Dave. He was not certain there was anything to say to his father either, but he would have liked at least to listen to him. He waited for his mother to look up and motion him into the booth, but he did not really expect to be called. He knew there were things he could not be trusted to keep quiet about. It was complicated. It would not just be a boy talking to his father; it would never be just that anymore.

At some point the balloon simply burst. The string dropped and coiled on his hand, and a red flap of rubber plopped on top of it. Dave looked up. So did his mother, and he saw her mouth slacken for a second, then resume speaking. Asa continued to hold the string and rubber; he liked the color better this way.

His mother hung up the phone and came out of the booth. She gave a quick smile to Dave, raising her eyebrows, and a longer smile to Asa. She said, "Your father says he knows now that what we've done is best, because that's the first time a balloon of yours has popped and you haven't cried. He says he knows now you have grown up a lot today." She regarded him proudly, as if everything in the world had been suddenly settled.

They went back to the bungalows. Dave saw

them to their door, and as Asa was stepping through the doorway, he stuck out his hand, to shake. Asa paused, then moved his string and rubber to his left hand and shook. Dave said, "Never mind getting back on the horse, Sport," and went to his own bungalow. He did not say good night to Asa's mother.

There were two beds. Asa fell asleep in one of them before his mother had even turned out the light. He slept hard and did not dream. Some time later, he woke up.

It was dark in the bungalow, except for a thin line of light on one edge of the curtain over the small window. Asa listened for his mother's breathing. He heard only his own. No one else was there.

His eyes adjusted to the dark, and he got up. The sheet on his mother's bed was turned down. In the middle of the mattress on the side near Asa's bed was a round depression, where he supposed she had sat and watched him sleep. Asa found his clothes and got dressed in the dark. He found his mother's purse and felt around inside for a couple of bills, which he put in his pocket.

93-126

He peeked past the edge of the curtain. The porch light was on. The macadam in front of the bungalow was clear. Quietly he opened the door and slipped out, closing it after him. Without a glance at number 10, he trotted off down the drive.

He found his way by working toward the glow of lights hanging out over the ocean. The streets were quiet, but the boardwalk still held a stream of people. They were different people this time: slower, without so many prizes and desserts, walking straighter, as if they were looking for something. He thought the aimless people he had seen earlier were all in bed now.

As he passed through the arch at the pier's entrance he noticed the red coating was flaking off the surfaces of the small bulbs, and something stirred in his memory, but he did not stop to think. He ran between the rides, most of which were motionless now, out to the end of the pier and the platform for the roller coaster. The man with the tattoos was still there, still leaning. His pencil was gone; he smoked a cigarette instead.

He arched his eyebrows when Asa stepped up and held out his bills. The man watched him for a second, then said, "What the hell," and took them, putting them in a pants pocket. He made the same backhanded wave as before, and Asa followed it.

He took the same car. He pulled the bar down himself this time, and clicked the chain across the cutaway, before the man could even jump up onto the platform. This time he did not watch the man reach into the dark machine and extract the huge lever; he knew what was happening, there was nothing new to see. He stared straight ahead at the sky and the slanting black water, which looked exactly the same as it had before. And as the engine kicked into gear and his car shot forward, he realized the peeling red light bulbs reminded him of radishes, and he had to try to remember that there had been some radishes that were *his* radishes. Had that been only *today*? As the car banked hard into the first turn, he realized the things he had left behind were already hiding inside him; now, for the first time, his life had a past, a past that would not get any bigger, that would always be shrinking but would never disappear. Something else: he had always assumed there was only one way for his life to happen. Now he realized there were alternatives. A feeling, an object, a person could seem like one thing but be another; an action could seem as if it were taking one turn, but veer off another way. Anything could happen at any time. He was not on tracks.

He pushed the chrome bar off his lap. The car swayed out over the edge of the pier, staying on its course by the tightest of tensions. Asa stood up straight into the warm wind and gathered his strength, as if to jump, as if to fly, as if, as if, as if.

ONE

STANDING IN THE DOORWAY, LOOKING IN PAST THE principal waiting to introduce him, Asa could see that his new fourth-grade class was just starting Rome. On one side of the room the boys were waving cardboard swords and wooden spears with tinfoil points; on the other side, the girls were wrapping themselves in white bedsheets. It had to be Rome. In his previous school they had already whipped through this part of history. But glancing around the room, he sensed a big difference here, a difference that gave him a little boost of excitement. The spears and togas, the number of fat books in the bookcases, the radiant messiness of wild drawings on the art bulletin board, the absence of the cardboard flashcards showing how the alphabet was formed in cursive—these were all good signs. Asa could tell about a classroom's spirit almost by sniffing the air. Mrs. Brock, a short, plump, young woman who had waved at the principal and finished fastening a spearpoint before coming over, was going to be fine.

In his previous fourth grade the teacher had not been very good. She would not have dared to split the class up this way into groups. And swords? Never. They had spent two days sitting in their five rows of six desks, talking only about the splendor of Roman banquets, as if the entire civilization had been based on eating a lot while lying down. The other teacher had also been pretty bad at bringing Asa into the class, though he had arrived only four days after the beginning of the school year. She sagged when he came to the door, shaking her head at the rows of neatly occupied desks. He knew she did not dislike him; she was just not up to the task of stirring a new kid into her stew. That's how it usually was: Two teachers in the second grade, two in the third, and now he was on his second in the fourth: he felt sorry for them all. He wanted to reassure them, the first time he appeared at the doors of their classrooms in the middle of a lesson—he wanted to tell them it was okay if they just let him be: he would find a way in all by himself, just far enough in to satisfy everyone, and then before long he would be gone.

Mrs. Brock glanced a quick smile at him, then gave her attention to the principal. It was a good smile that said *Let's get this official guy out of the way and we'll have plenty of time to get together*. Asa exhaled silently with relief.

As soon as the principal withdrew, Mrs. Brock pulled Asa into the room and guided him over to the huddle of boys. A waft of soft perfume rose warmly from the arm that lay across his shoulders. "All right," she said, handing him a sword, "you'll be—let's see—oh, Antonius. Thursday you and these three senators will present a report to the tribunal on the prospects for war with Carthage. You be the one to talk about the elephants, okay? Okay, guys?"

"I was going to do the elephants," said a large boy with a thick shirt, eyeing Asa.

"Then you do the weapons of Carthage now, Mark," said Mrs. Brock. "You're the wicked type, so that ought to keep you happy. Do pikes and hooks and scimitars and whatever else the Carthaginians planned on sticking into your flabby pink Roman rib cage. Have you," she said, turning to Asa with what he could only recognize as brilliant intuition, "ever seen an elephant?"

"African or Indian?" he said. He blushed, ashamed of showing off, for he had seen both in the National Zoo.

"Lord help us, a smarty-pants," she said, turning away to go rewrap the girls in togas.

"So," said Mark, pointing at Asa with his sword and bringing him across the threshold of the class with the easy nature of the threat, "you better give us a good idea what we should use to *kill* those suckers."

He did. His report a few days later stunned them all. Oh, Asa knew how to make the most of an opportunity for debut. He was aware that every time he came to a new class he had the chance to create himself in the eyes of the strangers with whom he would spend the next little while—a chance the hometown kids never got, being familiar with each other since the beginning of kindergarten or earlier. Asa, by now, knew what kind of attention would be aimed at him, knew which aspects of curiosity to exploit and which to deflect. He was good. He could put on a show.

In the middle of the tribunal presentation he unfurled huge drawings done on the floor of his bedroom on sheets of manila paper, taped together to twelve times the usual size—strangely colored drawings of grotesque exaggerations of elephants as they might have been imagined by Romans who had, after all, never seen one. He struck a senatorial tone that vacillated between military bravado and fascinated fear, emphasizing with wonder the fabulous violence that could be wrought by these wild things driven by wild men. He finished with a roaring challenge to the citizens to "see to our defenses lest we be torn, gored, and rent asunder by the ravaging fury of unknown forces not so distant in time and place!" The boys rose spontaneously to their feet with a roar, shaking their weapons defiantly, devotedly. The girls stared, impressed; they could appreciate a good report. One girl later asked soberly where he had acquired the archaic language. He confessed it was from the Bible. She nodded thoughtfully.

Even before his debut Asa had found ways into and out of the needs and enthusiasms of quite a few of his classmates. Steve was afraid of being stupid; so when talking to Steve, he used words that were long but common, and left sentences unfinished, groping for a word Steve could leap to provide. Cheryl liked to laugh at things no one else would find funny, so Asa dotted their talks with quirky details and reacted with a surprised thrill when she cackled. Lee was a comic-book freak who mystified other kids by comparing the subject of every conversation to some obscure subplot from a superhero tale, which he related with awkward, rushed specificity. Asa, who knew all the subplots, brightened Lee's eyes by providing a detail here and there (and a crisp translation, for Lee's confused listeners).

Everyone had an opening. Finding it only took alertness. As for slipping through the openings—well, it just seemed to happen. Asa was not being artificial or even artful. He did not pretend or dupe. With Steve, for example, it seemed he really *couldn't* think of that missing word, though at another time he had words by the hundreds to fill every blank. It was all managed above anyone's notice. This gave the illusion of naturalness, even, sometimes, to Asa himself.

After Rome was finished, he imagined he had made up for the weeks lost at the beginning of the year, if not for the years lost from kindergarten on. He had roles; he could be counted on for certain things. On the playground he had shown what he could do with the various tops, yo-yos, pocketknives, and harmonicas that demanded demonstrations of proficiency from every boy, in every school. Though he had never been anywhere long enough to learn team sports, when it came to portable skills, he could *play*. In the classroom his strengths had come out clearly, too, as he was called on for this and that. He could be counted on to whip through big-number multiplications and divisions in his head with an arrogant immediacy. And his long sentences—which filled themselves in as they wound their way around the subject of a question, opening impossible challenges of tense and sense in their early clauses but always, always coming to a brilliant conclusion—became a kind of group exercise in suspense and release as everyone felt the momentum pick up, heard the possibilities for error accrue, kept track of the bits that would be required for final resolution, and applauded with laughter as he boisterously provided them. He would have bet that his classmates, if asked about him, would not have recalled in their first thought, or even their fifth, that he had been inserted into the class six weeks into the year.

So it was something of a shock when Mrs. Brock clapped her hands one afternoon early in his third week and said, "All right, my little prima donnas, we've been taking it easy, but now it's time to rehearse for Show Night," and everyone separated into configurations he had never seen, twos, fives, boys with girls, singletons. He stood at his desk, blinking, uncertain. Right away Mrs. Brock noticed him, and put her hands on her cheeks in mock horror.

"Asa, what a chucklehead I am," she said. "I completely forgot."

She explained that every year the PTA kicked off its membership drive in the late fall with a variety show put on by a single class. This year was the fourth grade's turn. During the second week of school, each child had chosen something to do for the show. Six of them together were enacting a play they had written about the first Thanksgiving. Two others were putting together a clown act, in which, she suspected, they planned to throw a few of the pies used as props by the earlier pilgrims. One girl was dressing up as Robert E. Lee and giving short speeches about how the South actually had won the Civil War. What, she asked, did Asa want to do?

What *did* Asa want to do? Well, his project had been making friends, his concentration so keen that, at this moment, he was unable to think of himself doing something alone.

It did not take Mrs. Brock long to sense that he was at a loss. She motioned to the three solo acts, two boys and the girl who would be Robert E. Lee. They came over. "Okay," she said. "Who wants a partner? Amy Louise?"

"Mrs. Brock I cannot possibly," said the girl, clearly offended, perhaps by the implication that Robert E. Lee could be joined as an equal by anyone, or perhaps by the implication that she herself could.

"Fine. Generals can be very difficult colleagues anyway, Asa," said Mrs. Brock. "How about you, Harold?"

Harold looked confused. He often did. "It ain't nothing but radio," he said.

"Of course, of course." Mrs. Brock patted his shoulder. "Harold is a ham radio nut. His performance is to set up his receiver and pull in a broadcast from Russia. Very exciting, but not the sort of thing that invites collaboration. Well, Joel?"

Joel was a tall boy with fuzzy hair and a red face, all the parts of which seemed to be straining outward in a parody of aggressive friendliness toward all: his eyes popped, his nose arched, his cheeks bulged, even his teeth seemed to reach. He had spoken to Asa often, especially in his first days in the class; he had even invited the new boy over to play at his house after school two or three times. Asa had not been much interested; he had more challenging conquests to mount. Now, at the prospect of sharing, Joel was about to burst with goodwill.

"Mrs. Brock, Asa would be welcome to recite with me." He shifted his grin to Asa and held out a very old book.

"Joel is going to recite a poem," she explained. As Asa made no move, she took the book herself and thumbed through it. "Something by Eugene Field, wasn't it?"

Joel nodded. "'Little Boy Blue,'" he said. "Not the nursery rhyme with the 'come blow your horn' stuff. *This* is a really neat poem. We can say it together, if you like. That would be fun. We can practice so we match. Like the Everly Brothers."

Mrs. Brock winced slightly. "That might, well, be a little *much*, boys. I mean, two voices in unison would sort of draw attention away from the—the lonesome sadness of the single child passing away, you see. Break up the effect. But maybe you could alternate stanzas. . . ." She held the book out to Asa. He had no choice but to take it.

"Sure!" said Joel.

Asa frowned into the text. "Well," he heard himself say, "okay. Thanks."

At home, in his room alone, he thought of a dozen things he would rather do for the show than recite a poem called "Little Boy Blue" with Joel. Each inspired him to get up and go to the telephone. He even looked up Mrs. Brock's number. *Look*, he would tell her, *I want to juggle large chrome rings*, or *I want to present the calls of twenty birds*, or *I want to play my guitar*. He would make a point of sounding very simply excited, as if Joel did not enter into it at all, as if his own sheer creativity were driving him to nix the deal he had made that afternoon.

The only thing that made Asa pause before dialing Mrs. Brock's number was the fact that he could not juggle, he could not imitate the calls of birds, he owned no guitar. There was no doubt in his mind that he could scramble and master one of these tasks by the time he needed to perform; he could do anything he thought of doing, he was certain. But Joel had told him Mrs. Brock asked the other students to give a quick demonstration of their tricks so that she could approve or redirect their showmanship. In fact, she had suggested that two of them make changes: Susan, a haughty, religious girl, had wanted to sing three Baptist hymns; but she could not carry a tune, so she was now slated to recite three psalms; and Peter, whose voice-and-gesture impressions of John Wayne, President Eisenhower, and Ed Sullivan had all seemed exactly alike, was now going to sing "The Yellow Rose of Texas" and "The Streets of Laredo" while dressed as a cowboy. *However*, Joel reported with ecstasy, *however*, Asa was approved without audition to recite "Little Boy Blue." Imagine! Well, Asa, who had a feeling Mrs. Brock knew she was taking a pretty slim risk in letting him mumble a few lines unapproved, did not want to test that faith. He had a feeling it would not extend to juggling and birdcalls.

He sat in his room looking out the window. Outside, the moon sat high and round and white in the dense, dark sky. The moon was isolated, touching nothing, having no effect on the darkness around it; it seemed as if any minute the vastly greater darkness would simply take over, and the moon would be no more. Yet down in his backyard a small apple tree was casting a thick shadow on the lawn. The shadow was there because the tree was standing in the way of the moonlight, which shone bright as lightning on everything in sight. How could this be? How could the moonlight get all the way here through the sky without leaving some silver trace? Asa felt his curiosity and intelligence quicken, and he knew he could figure it out in time, and after he did, he would love moonlight. From insight to love was not a big step.

This is what he was good at, he realized. This is what he *did*. He placed himself in the world, and the world drew his thoughts outside himself, where they multiplied and spiraled and led him in silent, thrilling flights. And as he expanded into the world, he expanded inside. At these moments an endlessness beyond thought opened inside him. Outside, his mind was whizzing through things, but inside, he was silent, still; sometimes, he knew he was not even breathing.

How do you put on a show of *that*? Asa felt that these abilities and experiences must appear, some-how, in everything he did, in what he *was*; but how could anyone be expected to know what he was? He was alone. That was it, really. Even when he was scurrying around figuring the angles and openings of other people, he was operating alone.

He was a singleton, not a showman.

He got up from the window and found Joel's book. He thought of taking it back to the window and reading it by the moonlight, but he could not do it—not a poem called "Little Boy Blue." The ghost of Eugene Field was probably hovering somewhere *begging* him to read it in the moonlight, then cry silver tears. He switched on his overhead light.

He found the poem and read it. When he finished, he stared at the wall. It was difficult to believe that someone had written this. He read it again, and this time, he found it difficult to believe that someone else, even a kid, had chosen it to recite, on a stage, in front of other people. A sweet little boy pats his stuffed animals and drops dead in the night, and oh what a sad, sad world it is. Asa tried to laugh, but found that despite his scorn, he could not easily shake the heavy sadness the poem labored so shamelessly to create. This made him furious.

A few months ago, he and his mother and stepfather had been at a restaurant. While they were waiting for their food, Dave had gotten up and gone to the jukebox. He studied the selections for a moment, dropped in a coin, and pressed two buttons. A song bloomed from the small speaker over their booth, a song his mother apparently recognized, for as Dave sat down again next to Asa, she looked across at him and said, "Oh, honey, thanks."

The song was sung by a man with a high, rather nasal voice. It was a personal narrative about his darling young wife. She had come to him one spring, they had been in love for a year, then for some reason—something woeful that happened between the second chorus and the third verse, during the violin solo—she died. In the last verse, he was looking at a tree in the yard and noticing that it had grown. She, of course, being dead, had not, which (Asa thought) must be what made his mother so sad. For she was crying by the time the violins—hundreds of them by now—faded back into the speaker.

They sat in silence, except for his mother's snufflings. Asa said nothing. The air at the table was suddenly very tense; there was danger popping like ions. Asa would not have spoken for a hundred dollars. He held his breath and hoped the food would come. He saw the waitress emerge from the kitchen, carrying a tray with three plates. He let his breath out as she approached. He had made it.

But then, just before she arrived, Dave held up a hand to stop her. He turned his head slightly and looked sideways at Asa with a thin, amused smile. "Well?" he said.

Asa stared at the waitress. She stood, holding the heavy tray. "Well what?" the boy said, innocently.

Dave lifted his chin in a little nod at him. The smile held. "Well, what did you think of the song?"

Asa looked at his stepfather. Across the table, his mother had sniffed to a halt, and was wiping her eyes with a napkin. "I'm hungry," the boy said. "Please let's just eat."

The waitress made a move to put the tray down, but Dave held his hand out again and stopped her. "Now, I think it's a fair question to ask a boy, don't you? Just a simple question. And a boy ought to answer when he's spoken to." He lifted his chin again, and the smile tightened. "So answer me, unless you want to be reminded of your manners when we get home."

Asa took a deep breath and tried to hold it. He couldn't hold it forever. "All right," he burst out, louder than he wanted to be. "Okay. It's a stupid song designed to suck the easy stupid sad feelings out of people who have plenty of other things to feel sad about, and it's about as real as the sunshine in cigarette commercials, and I hate *every stinking word*."

He sat, breathing hard and quaking, his eyes bulging hard against the insides of his eyelids with every pounding heartbeat, making the restaurant disappear in flashes of white, white, white. His mother exploded into sobs once more, but worse this time: real. Dave apparently gave the waitress a signal, for she now began to place the food in front of them. Asa stared down at his plate of spaghetti and said, "I have to get up. I'm going to be sick." Dave did not move to let him out of the booth, but leisurely stuck his fork into his own spaghetti, and twirled until a large mass hung on the end. This he raised until it was just in front of his face. He studied it. Asa's mother wailed across the table.

Dave said, "Well, yes. I guess—I guess you have to have a *heart* to like that song. Not just a brain."

Now, it seemed, Asa would once again have to make public his heartlessness: he hated every word of "Little Boy Blue," which, probably, all other human beings on the planet adored, and unless he wanted to recite "And that was the time when our Little Boy Blue/Kissed them and put them there" about a toy dog and a tin soldier, he would have to say so.

Before he knew it, he was standing on his bed. He bounced up and came down, hard. This was forbidden; Dave and his mother could hear in their bedroom below. It was sure to bring Dave up, scowling and storming. "'Now don't you go till I come,'" Asa recited loudly, bouncing again, "'And don't you make any *noise*!'" He bounced one, two, three times, found a comfortable rhythm, *bowm, bowm, bowm, bowm.*

"'And toddling off to his trundle bed,'" Asa shouted, "'He dreamt of the pretty toys.' Hoo boy!

Are those poor little toys in for a big *surprise*!" He cackled and lifted his knees, dropping even deeper into the mattress, *whong!*, springing even higher. Again he laughed, louder and wilder, and as long as his mouth was open and his voice sounded good, why not go ahead and holler this stupid poem that seemed to have stuck in his memory after only two readings? So he launched into a full-blown recitation, emphasizing the special moments of pathos with hoots or moans; except for a line or two (which he filled in by singing "Blue-d'dee blue-d'dee" *bowm, bowm, bowm*) he had the whole thing by heart. He built up to a big finish by bouncing higher, shouting louder, higher, louder, higher . . . until he arrived at the end and sprang spread-eagled off his bed out into the air of his room, singing "What has become of our Little Boy Blue?" in falsetto as he soared. Then his heels hit the floor with a stunning jolt, and he sprawled. He lay there, panting, waiting.

From below there was no sound. That was odd. He sat up, still panting. What was the matter down there? Perhaps they were weeping with the sadness of it all. Poor Little Boy Blue! Maybe they'd like to hear it again. He got up and found the book, intending to brush up on the couple of lines he'd blown. He snatched it open and scratched roughly through the pages, looking for the poem, intending to read it aloud with volume and sarcasm. He held the text up close to his face.

It was not "Little Boy Blue"; he was on the wrong page. But before he could flip it, he had read a line or two, and he stopped. The lines were "And dark in the dark old inn-yard a stable wicket creaked/Where Tim the ostler listened; his face was white and peaked."

Asa read the lines again. He didn't know what an ostler was. He didn't even know what a stable wicket was. But he knew they were better than toy dogs and tin soldiers, and he knew above all that when an ostler with a white, peaked face listened by a creaking wicket dark in a dark old inn-yard, something was afoot. He read the next lines: "His eyes were hollows of madness, his hair like moldy hay/But he loved the landlord's daughter/The landlord's red-lipped daughter,/Dumb as a dog he listened,/And he heard the robber say . . ."

Now, thought Asa, springing up with the book

in his hand and shaking a fist, *now* by God we are *onto* something. Just ahead of his thoughts he saw a solution to his problem, he saw poor Little Boy Blue dying alone and unsung in the darkness far from voice and stage, but at the moment he did not want to think it through. To heck with Little Boy Blue. He wanted to *read*. So, quietly, he turned out his overhead light, and quietly pulled a chair into the moonlight coming through his window.

T W O

"'A COAT OF THE CLARET VELVET,'" CAME JOEL'S VOICE over his shoulder, "'and boots of the brown doe-skin.'"

"No," said Asa, stopping on the leafy path. "No. Not boots, and not '*the* brown doe-skin.' It's his *breeches* that are made of that: 'breeches of brown doe-skin.'" As an afterthought he added, "You had the right sense of the rhythm, though. You added that 'the' to make up for the difference in syllables between 'boots' and 'breeches.'"

Joel had stopped now too, and he came walking back, snapping a withering leaf shaped like a mitten from a sassafras bush. "I forget what breeches are again," he said. He stuck the leaf's stem in his mouth.

"Pants," said Asa. Every time they went over this, he was tempted to mention the obvious clue; but he was afraid that if he called Joel's attention to the similarity between the familiar word "britches" and the unknown word, Joel would just start saying "britches." He supposed that would be better than "boots," but he hated the way it sounded.

Joel twirled the leaf in front of his face by rolling the stem between his pink lips. The leaf fell. "You know why I can never remember that? Because it doesn't make any sense. I mean, doeskin is like leather, right? Well, whoever heard of leather *pants*?"

Asa sighed, and sat on a fallen tree trunk. "It's very soft," he said. "Doeskin I mean. It's as soft as cashmere."

"How do you know?" Joel asked, taking a seat up the trunk from Asa. There was no challenge in his voice, Asa knew; Joel didn't doubt, he just wondered.

"My mother has some doeskin gloves."

"Ah." Joel looked around, sighed contentedly, and began to whistle. Asa said nothing. He felt bad for an instant; his mother had never had doeskin gloves, at least as far as he knew. He had lied.

"Shall we try it again?" he asked.

"You know," said Joel, "you are the only kid I ever knew who actually says things like 'shall.' Is it because you're a Yankee?"

"I'm not a Yankee," Asa said patiently. "Washington is below the Mason-Dixon line."

"May be," said Joel, "but it's a big city. Seems like all big cities are Yankee, really."

"What about Atlanta?"

"Well, I guess you got me there." Joel stood up and stretched slowly, smiling at the woods all around. "You got to admit," he said, "that this is better than a stuffy room."

"Yes, it is," said Asa. "But the reason we stopped working in my room was that you said you couldn't learn anything in there but you could learn *anything* outside." He paused, then added:

"It's only a week away, Joel."

"I know," Joel said, with a heavy sigh Asa hoped was faked for his benefit. "I'm not doing too very good."

"You're doing fine," Asa said, "but you just need to speed up."

"And you gave me all the hot verses."

"Stanzas," said Asa. It was true: in an effort to engage Joel's enthusiasm, and thereby his concentration, Asa had abandoned their initial scheme of simple alternation, coming up instead with an arrangement that favored Joel with the exciting parts. Joel was now responsible for telling the audience about the moon being a ghostly galleon, about Tim the ostler's white peaked face, about the brave robber with the twinkling pistol butts rising in the saddle to kiss his bonny sweetheart while his face burnt and her perfumed hair tumbled all over him, and, best of all, about the gallant, galloping fellow turning back on the murderous redcoats, shrieking a curse to the sky with the white road smoking behind him and his rapier brandished high. But instead of rising to the thrill of this amazing privilege, Joel scattered his attention at every strange, marvelous old word, unable to keep his ostlers and rapiers and breeches straight. He still couldn't really grasp why they called a robber a "highwayman." He said it sounded like a highwayman ought to be a guy doing road work.

The switch hadn't worked, but Asa wasn't willing after two weeks of effort to undo whatever odd bits of memorization Joel had accomplished by reclaiming the choice stanzas for himself. Besides, he was still deeply grateful for the easygoing way Joel had agreed to drop "Little Boy Blue" and take on the much longer poem. Sometimes, though, he was tempted to wish for a way he could recite the whole thing himself.

Joel had started walking back in the direction of the house; it appeared that today's rehearsal was about to end. Asa shook his head, and fell into step behind the larger boy.

After a few minutes, Joel asked, "Do you think I'll make it?"

Without thinking, Asa said, "Yes."

"I don't. I'm sorry I'm so dumb."

"You're not dumb."

"I had 'Little Boy Blue' down *cold*."

Asa doubted this; he doubted Joel had his own telephone number down cold; but he only said, "I know. It was tough on you to switch."

"It's worth it," said Joel brightly. "We're better friends because we have to work so hard on this one."

Asa doubted this, too. He hated to doubt it, but he did. While it was true that he had changed his mind about Joel—coming to appreciate the boy's open-minded readiness to like anyone or try anything with a full heart and reckless energy, at the slightest encouraging sign—he had been unable to slip into the relaxed carelessness of friendship. Joel needed too much handling for that. The responsibilities Asa had to adopt toward him simply prevented spontaneity, trust—equality. The role was set. He was Joel's manager.

The week zipped away. Joel missed two of their daily practice sessions, once so that he could work on a tree house his younger brother was building in their backyard. Asa called him on the phone and complained. Joel said, "But I promised him I'd help. It was a deal."

"What about your deal with me?"

Joel thought about it. "It's different. See, I'm not *helping* you. The guy who's doing the *helping*, it's, it's like—"

"I know," said Asa drily.

"Sure," said Joel, "I guess you do. And, boy, do I know what a good helper *you* are. You're my idol when it comes to helping, believe me." He laughed. "Anyway," he added casually, "he's my brother, see."

"That," said Asa, despising himself, even as he spoke, for the obvious self-pity, "is of course something I know *nothing* about," and he hung up softly.

Later that night, Joel called him back and recited twelve new lines, making no mistakes. Asa praised him gratefully. He also suspected that perhaps Joel had been reading to him—not in the spirit of cheating, for Joel was not deceitful, but to make Asa happy. He wished the idea of Joel fudging had not been so automatic, but there it was.

The next day at school Joel was as bright and breezy as ever, and Asa was contrite. He suggested that they make up for the missed time by pounding through two tremendous sessions over the weekend. Joel agreed happily. So, on Saturday morning, Asa made lemonade and baked a whole sheet of chocolate-chip cookies, while his mother assembled two huge submarine sandwiches, her specialty. Everything was cooling in the refrigerator when the telephone rang. Asa answered.

"*Tlot-tlot*," said a dramatic voice.

"Hi man," Asa said, looking at the clock. Joel was due in ten minutes. Obviously, he would be late. "What's up?"

"Hey, what's up is just the question to ask. What's *up*, what's *way* up, is the tree house. We finished it. Right now it's swarming with second graders, but guess who reserved it for a solid hour this afternoon, so we can practice our robbers and red-coats?"

"You're supposed to come here. You're—you're supposed to *be* here. Now! For *three* hours. What's the matter with you? Are you crazy?"

"An hour in a tree house is worth three in a stuffy old room any day. Come on. Get your mom to bring you. We can scare the little guys and stuff. It'll be fun."

So Asa packed his knapsack with the subs and cookies and a thermos of the lemonade. Dave was off with the car, playing golf, so he had to ride his bicycle. Joel lived five or six miles across town, in an area of fine old houses that seemed as big as ships to Asa. It took him almost an hour to get there, and the only thing that kept him from pumping with anger was the chance to pretend that he was himself the highwayman, narrating his own harsh and noble deeds with the wind in his teeth.

After arriving at Joel's house and parking his bike, he headed toward the sounds of wild hooting and howling far behind the house. From fifty feet away he saw the tree house, about twelve feet up in a big beech. Around the trunk were eight or ten younger kids, looking up and yelling, jumping and shaking knotty little fists. Most of them were quite wet. As he watched, Joel's head and shoulders suddenly shot up over one wall made of an old tin sign bearing a peeling portrait of the Sinclair gasoline brontosaurus. Joel's face was a beaming, bursting cartoon expression of devilish delight at finding the young kids beneath him; he wagged his eyebrows and shook his hair and roared, and the kids howled back and started laughing in fright and pleasure. At just the right moment, when it seemed they would all incinerate with happy dread, he stood up tall and began lofting water balloons at them. Wobbling in their arcs like live things, the balloons—shiny green, blue, red, yellow—caught sunlight in their watery interiors and held it in a glow. Then each of them exploded on the head or shoulders of a shrieking second grader.

Asa found he was crying. He left unseen.

THREE

His mother called him to the telephone. The caller was an adult woman with a rich Carolina accent who identified herself with her entire name, then added that she was Joel's mother.

"Ah," said Asa. "Hello."

"Asa," said the woman rather musically, "I'm sure you know why I'm calling."

"Well, not exactly." He hesitated, then said innocently, "Perhaps it's something to do with the presentation Joel and I are making tomorrow night?"

"You're sweet to be so optimistic, son."

"Ma'am?"

"Now, Asa, bright as you must be, I'm sure I don't have to spell it out for you. I'm well aware of what you've been trying to do for my Joel, so I know *you're* aware of—well, let's see—shall we say, the peculiar nature of the dear boy's intellectual gifts."

"Ma'am?"

"My, you *are* going to make me pull the flag all the way up the pole, aren't you? Look, my dear. Joel is full of sweetness and light, he was born full of sweetness and light, he'll live to be a hundred and the angels will be waiting for him with robes of gold, *but*—as his father and I and his teachers and I suspect you too know—while he's on this earth Joel could not find his own fanny with both hands. He is as close to helpless as you can get without being put on a leash. I love him more than any human since Clark Gable, but honey, let's be frank: when it come to little things like time and space and words and numbers, Joel is missing something between the I. and the Q."

"You're telling me he hasn't memorized his part of 'The Highwayman.'"

"See? I *told* you you were bright. Indeed, Joel has not memorized his part of that dreadful endless poem you two lit on reciting." She sighed dramatically. "We had him all set up with something simpler, which was hard enough, mind you—and it took him a week to remember what color 'Little Boy Blue' was, but we got almost all of it memorized somehow. Then you come along, all good intentions I'm sure, and of course it *is* a much finer piece of writing, but my God! it's long as a catfish's old age. He was all excited and eager to try it, and, of course, he looks on you as something between Mickey Mantle and Jesus. I couldn't tell him no—it's hard to keep saying no when he wants to try something, and the child is eat up with gumption—so I held my breath and prayed you were the kind of young man you've turned out to be. He's told me. You've been a saint. You understand him. But I can't help noticing you've given up your practices, and I wonder what you're thinking now about tomorrow."

Well, Asa had been wondering that himself. She was right: since his visit that Saturday, he had not tried to schedule any practice sessions with Joel. They had talked in class, Joel always eager to speak a couple of lines to show his readiness—*tlot-tlot!*—and Asa always complimentary and encouraging. But he had given up. Joel was on his own. Asa figured their part of the show would be a disaster.

On the surface, in the daylight of his public self, he had accepted this. On the surface, he was calm, resigned, cool. But just out of view, in the shadows where the real thinking was done, his scheming mind spent every hour trying to figure out a way to dump Joel and do it all himself. This was awful of him, but he could not stop wishing: maybe Joel will get chicken pox, maybe Joel will get stage fright, maybe Joel will move to Nebraska. Asa told himself he wasn't wishing like this for his own sake. Somehow, he felt, it was just for the sake of the poem itself, and the act of reciting it. There simply was a right way to do it, and when there was a right way, it should be done. It was as if there were a perfect movie of this event floating in the air somewhere in advance, and it was up to him to match it, word for word, motion for motion.

Now, on the phone with this odd woman, he sensed something like opportunity opening up before him. It was coming, if he could play this right. He said, "Well, to tell you the truth, I was just kind of going to show up and see what happened."

"Ha." She was silent for a moment. "Am I correct, Asa, in assuming that you know this entire poem, all by yourself?"

Carefully, as innocent as possible, he said, "Well—yes, I guess I do."

"You *guess* you do, do you. I get the feeling maybe you're about three curves ahead of me here, but you'd just as soon I did the suggesting, so I will. Here's what I think. I think Joel ought to kind of miss the big show and leave you to struggle bravely on. What do you think about that?"

"I think he'd feel terrible."

"Well, that's nice, but if I took care of things just

right, it would probably be a week before he even remembered, and then it would be so far gone, he'd tend to regard it as a pleasant memory of what might have been. Even if he faced it straight up, he wouldn't get too low about missing out; he snaps back faster than a fat man's suspenders, Joel does."

"Well . . ." said Asa. And he let her talk him into it. She had it all worked out: she would give Joel the day off from school, and they would go out and buy a football he wanted, then eat lunch at his favorite restaurant, then take in a submarine movie that was playing downtown—"Just a good old day of a boy and his momma being sweet on each other." She'd make sure his father and brother didn't mention anything about the show at dinner, after which they'd have a checkers tournament. That was Joel's favorite family activity, she said; he played the three of them at once on three boards, and murdered them.

He let her talk. And as she talked, he tested every seam of her plan, first figuring whether or not it would fool Joel, and then whether or not it would hurt him. In his head, the plan worked. Joel would be fooled; and as far as pain went—well, she knew Joel better than he, didn't she? Okay: Joel would not know. Okay: Joel would not be hurt. Okay. Okay.

He would do it alone.

F O U R

ONSTAGE, TWO GIRLS WERE DANCING IN TAFFETA costumes. One of them had been allowed to wear makeup, and she was dancing much better than her friend, whose pale face was streaked with the trail of dried tears; she had been forbidden to "doll up," and her misery threw her steps off. In the wings, boys were laughing as the pale girl stumbled. Asa watched, sympathetic.

From his position in the dark he could see out into the auditorium, across a band of the audience slanting from the front row to the rear. He did not recognize anyone, but he had guessed the identities of a few groups by seeing how they perked up as particular performers took the stage. His mother

and Dave were out there somewhere. Asa did not
know where they were sitting; they had dropped
him off early, gone out for Chinese food, and come
back in time for the show. Asa had gone to "green
room," which was what Mrs. Brock called their
classroom tonight. Everyone was in there, the girls
squealing and fidgeting, the boys looking pointedly disdainful and nervous. Mrs. Brock, wearing
a shiny blue dress and rather more makeup than
usual herself, darted from one performer to the
next with quizzes, reminders, stagecraft tips. After
everyone knew without exception to lick his lips,
to hold her chin up, to look straight into the audience without actually focusing on a face, fifteen
minutes remained before they could take their
places backstage. Everyone was too finely tuned
to relax, too close to fever to back coolly off, so after a couple of beats Mrs. Brock stood on a desk
and sang them songs in a perfect alto voice that
sounded as if it had been roasted. They were not
children's songs; the lyrics were full of desperate
inquiry about strange love, and the tunes mean-
dered like smoke from a slow-burning cigarette.
The children sat and stood, holding their juggling

stuff or their instruments, silent, wondering. The minutes passed. Finally Mrs. Brock closed a verse on a low, full note, hummed a whole chorus, and stopped. She looked at them as if she were some-where else. Then she smiled and said, "Songs by a lady named Holiday. Oooh—*sad* songs. Now, peo-ple, go to your places."

So far, most of the performances had been bet-ter than anyone could have hoped. Hands caught and tossed precisely, memories flashed, voices found a key and held it. Asa was amazed. Some-thing about the oddness of Mrs. Brock's im-promptu singing had cleared the nerves of his classmates. He had a feeling he too would be en-joying the same ebullience if his nervousness merely came from the prospect of standing up in front of a bunch of adults and doing something ar-tificial. But his nervousness was different. He was thinking about Joel.

Asa was worried that of all the performances onstage tonight, his would be the only one with consequences that stretched into the future. He knew hurt feelings could last. And the more he thought about it, the more he was certain Joel would be hurt. What could his mother have been thinking? Or, more to the point, what could *he* have been thinking?

The ballet dancers finished with twin spins, each slashing the air with a satin foot held high and curved. The girl without makeup had recovered her enthusiasm toward the end of their dance: her last few steps were sharper, and her leaps higher, than those of her partner, and as they stood panting slightly, grinning at the audience's applause, her face shone with a pink radiance that shamed the powder and technique offered beside her. Asa, breaking the rules, clapped. The girl waiting to go on in front of him—Amy Louise, dressed in a baggy gray uniform that might have fit General Lee—turned in horror and shook her head. He stopped. The ballerinas curtsied twice and came off. In her joy, the second of them gave a flip to the velvet side curtain with her hand. Asa happened to be looking at her, and as the curtain swayed, it gave him a glimpse of the rear doors of the auditorium. In that instant, he saw Joel's mother dash in, looking distraught.

Amy Louise was already walking out toward

the center of the stage. In a second he overtook her, pulling her by the elbow and mumbling an apology as he passed. She took one look at his face and turned back to the wings without a word.

He found himself standing in bright lights, facing perhaps 800 people. He looked past them to the back and located Joel's mother. She raised her hands at him and shook her head. Then she pointed at the back door. Then she held her hands as if she were riding a bicycle, and pointed at the back door. Once more she held up her hands as if helpless. Then, finally, urgently, she motioned him to start.

He nodded. From the wings he heard Mrs. Brock's voice: "Asa. What the dickens are you doing out there?" Asa realized she had not asked about Joel's absence; this meant she had been squared by Joel's mom. Asa did not look at her. Instead, he stepped up to the apron of the stage and lifted his chin.

"Good evening," he said. He noticed several people looking at their yellow mimeographed programs, noting he was out of order. He gave them a second to stop rustling. Then, just as his tongue touched his top teeth to make the first sound in announcing "'The Highwayman,' by Alfred Noyes," the same back door flew open and in ran Joel.

He was panting and his face was even redder than usual. He was wearing a blue blazer hitched back on his shoulders as if the wind were blowing down the back of his neck, a very wrinkled white shirt, and an orange clip-on tie fastened only on one side of the knot: his right leg had a rubber band around it at the ankle, to keep his good gray trousers out of his bicycle chain. His eyes shot to the stage and found Asa. Right away all the haste and tension left him, and he grinned: *Hey! I made it!* He gave a little wave and started to trot down the center aisle. But somewhere on the way another thought hit him and he stopped. This time, when he looked up at Asa, Joel wasn't grinning.

Asa had not moved; his expression had not changed. He took a quick reading of his own face and decided it showed surprise, and a frustration he was ashamed of, frozen there the instant Joel burst in. He knew it was clear, what he had been about to do. And it was too late to shift into some sort of welcoming smile now. So he kept Joel's eye straight on, and watched as his friend came to realize his treachery.

He saw Joel get it, reject the idea, then get it again. Joel looked around, and found his mother leaning against the back wall. In the auditorium, no one else moved or spoke; it was as if a sudden lightning storm were flashing incomprehensibly above their heads.

Joel swung his eyes back to Asa. And there, in those bright eyes, Asa watched the flutter of pain disappear, replaced in a flicker by cheery acquiescence. Joel smiled, a huge one, genuine, frank, full of acceptance of himself and the strategies necessary to get around him; he shrugged, gestured for Asa to go on. Then he looked down the rows to his left for a seat.

From the wings, Mrs. Brock now said, "Go ahead, Asa. Go on, now." Asa swallowed. He looked around the auditorium, taking in the expectant faces. One of them was Joel's, already watching him with the same expression of readiness to be thrilled. The quick lightning storm was over. Showtime.

"Good evening," he repeated. His voice was thin; he swallowed, licked his lips, took a breath that felt like water. He looked at Joel. Joel nodded. "All right," Asa said. "Okay." He decided, and drew another breath. This one felt warm and dry. "Now. A change. The next item in the program was to have been a dual recitation of 'The Highwayman' by Alfred Noyes, performed by Joel Prescott and Asa Hill. There has been a change." He glanced around the room. The faces waited. "Instead of 'The Highwayman,' Joel and I will now recite 'Little Boy Blue' by Eugene Field. We think you will like it." He paused. "Joel?"

Joel was already hustling down the aisle, fingers at his tie, lips moving confidently over remembered words.

O N E

THE DEW WAS FALLING. ASA FROWNED AND SCUFFED the grass with his right foot. In twenty minutes it would be slick as wet tile. He sighed. This was the peril of playing in the second game of the evening: the dew always fell.

Far away at home plate, the batter swung. Asa jumped as he always did when the ball sprang off the bat. This time it was not sailing to him in center field; it lifted straight up in front of home plate. Asa kept moving anyway, his feet keeping pace with the choices his intuition made. He watched the catcher, looking straight up, spin and stagger in a rough circle as the ball peaked and began to drop. Asa trotted low and quiet along a curved shadow that ran between left and center, where the pools of light from the high spots did not quite meet.

The ball came down just as the catcher, in mid-step, was recovering from a dizzy half turn, two feet inside the first baseline. The ball glanced off the heel of his mitt like a waterfall off a rock. The kid who had hit it and run looked back as he rounded first. He hesitated a second while the catcher whirled his head around in confusion, looking for the ball the way a dog does when someone stands on it for a joke; then the runner lit out for second. The catcher found the ball, looked up, saw the runner, and, swaddled by his heavy gear and strained by his panic at the infielders' screams, unleashed a wild throw that disappeared into the black sky fifteen feet over the shortstop's head. The runner, grinning, kept right on running, around second, lightly and surely for third.

Forty feet beyond the shortstop, however, stood Asa, unnoticed. He hollered the third baseman's name, calmly caught the catcher's wild ball on the fly, turned, and fired it—tamed and orderly now—on one hop to third. The third baseman, alerted by the holler, caught it and neatly tagged the runner, who was so surprised by the sight of the ball arriving in front of him that he went into his slide six feet early and never even reached the base.

The umpire jerked his hand. The runner howled. Infielders strutted, slapped hands. The catcher, standing tall, jutted his jaw, jammed his mask on with a warning glare at the next batter, as if to say he hoped the kid had watched carefully and learned not to try to fox *him* with any twisty pop-ups. Asa trotted back to his position in center. Inside, his sense of right and wrong registered once again the justness of baseball: it was too fine a game to allow a triple off a dippy pop five feet from home plate.

The grass was wet now. Asa had to straighten his knees and jog on his heels, more upright, slower. He hated slowing down. Asa liked a challenge, but a dew slick was not a challenge. A challenge allowed solutions without sacrifices; adjustments, yes, but not sacrifices. Sacrificing speed was cheap and easy. *Anyone* could slow down.

The third batter of the inning swung too hard at an inside pitch and dribbled a grounder to the second baseman, who bobbled it but had plenty of time to throw it in the direction of first. The first baseman caught it, looked around for the bag, and stomped on it an instant before the runner arrived. Three outs. Time to bat.

Asa knew he batted fourth this inning; he could get his cuts if one of his teammates got on base. This, he also knew, was unlikely. It was equally unlikely that *he* would reach base when *his* turn came. The Quik-E-Freeze Cool Guys had not scored a single run in the first four games of the season.

Asa watched the boys assemble on the bench, rowdy and happy in relief that another spell amidst the mysteries of defense had somehow been brought to an end. For them, playing in the field was a bad dream—fielding frantic grounders that seemed to pick up speed as they kicked closer, and fly balls that vanished on the way up, only to reappear suddenly coming fast as cars; remembering which base to throw to when there was one out instead of two, or two on base instead of three. They tried to survive until the moment when three outs had miraculously accumulated, then— hooray!—it was off to the dugout to jostle and laugh and spray insect repellent in each other's ears until Coach told you you were on deck.

Mack and Jeff, who Asa knew were scheduled

to bat first and second this inning, sat along with the rest, waiting without a clue. Only Tim, the third baseman, up third, seemed to know his spot: his batting helmet was already on.

"Mack up, Jeff on deck, Timmy in the hole," said Coach Henderson. The boys scrambled eagerly. Asa listened for the slightest sound of disappointment in the coach's voice, but there was nothing but warmth and ease. He never seemed to expect them to keep up with the game. Watching him, you would think he barely paid attention himself: he seemed committed more to making the kids all feel good than to building a ball team.

Mack hit a line drive back to the pitcher. This boy, whose height and clear jawline revealed he was nearer 13 than 12 (the league's upper age limit), ducked and stuck up his mitt sideways without taking the extra second to try to open it for a catch. The ball caromed off the glove to the shortstop, who threw Mack out.

"Good hustle," said Coach Henderson as Mack returned, full of pep, no regrets, happy with the feel of the decent smack he had given the ball. Jeff stood in and the coach clapped. "Little bingle,

Jefferoo." Inspired, Jeff swung early at three high pitches in a row. Out two.

"Good cuts," said the coach.

"Yeah," said Jeff, eyes aglow. "I almost *fouled* that second one!"

"Attaboy." The coach and Asa watched Tim move out to the plate. Asa waited a moment, then stepped over to the on-deck circle.

He loved being on deck. He loved swinging two bats in a leisurely, patient way, as if this were all there was to it, lulling his arms to stretch and strengthen to handle the big weight. It was a trick, of course. When he went to the plate with only one bat and clicked into the quick intensity of the swing, his arms would find they were able to whip the wood around as if it were a hickory switch. It always worked: his arms never learned. This was a miracle to him—one part of him could remain innocent while another knew perfectly well what was happening.

He was delighted. All of this made him feel mysterious to himself, capable of doing things he could not foresee, with a power that reversed the usual cycle of observation, analysis, understanding, practice, action. *This* power came from *not* knowing, *not* understanding.

Tim took a couple of high ones, then scythed at a low pitch. The ball looped high over first and landed halfway out to right field, just on the line. The right fielder charged hard, scooped it up, and cocked his arm; but instead of firing a throw by instinct, he looked up at Tim rounding first. Tim was ready with a scowl that gave the fielder just a moment's uncertainty, and by the time the boy recovered, his throw was too late to beat Tim.

Good. Runner in scoring position. Asa clapped. He liked the way Tim played offense (though he was careless and impatient with his mitt on); now they might actually score a run, against all odds. The other team, Table Talk Bakery, was one of the best in the league. Their last game against Asa's team had ended 9–0, even with the Table Talk scrubs playing the final three innings.

Asa walked to the plate and took his stance. The Table Talk catcher, an ebullient All-Star named James Neal, chattered at him with a stream of good-natured taunts that were taunts nonetheless.

Asa ignored him and began what he called his

"checkup," going over his positioning limb by limb, using a special perception trick: he pretended he was his stepfather in the stands behind home plate. His stepfather *was* there, along with his mother; Asa knew this, though he never looked up at them during a game. And Asa knew his stepfather was scrutinizing his every move, holding the set of each elbow or eye against the technically determined ideal adopted when they practiced together. Dave knew *everything* about baseball, and was a patient, precise teacher. If Asa bent his knees too little, sat back on his heels too much, moved his head during the swing, or failed to roll his wrists all the way in his follow-through, he would hear about it next time they took the field together.

Now he was ready. The pitcher, looking bored, flipped a pitch that caught the outside corner in a hurry. His next one was in the dirt in front of the plate, and his third was high. Asa hated batting against a pitcher who wasn't taking the job seriously: it was impossible to fox someone who had no strategy. He stepped out of the batter's box, took a practice swing to refocus, then stepped back in. The pitcher, impatient, threw quickly.

The ball flicked toward the plate, and without deciding to swing Asa swung—it just looked like a good one. He hit it flush and it flew away. As he dropped the bat and ran, excitement fluttered in his chest. The ball soared high over center field; he willed it to keep going away, not to peak, not to begin its fall. He had never hit a home run; he had never hit a ball this hard. But as he touched first and watched, the ball faltered in its flight. He knew it would stay in the park—his center fielder's eye would not deceive him, no matter what his hopes. He kept running dutifully, in case of an error, but the excitement turned to a sigh. The outfielder, running back, slowed, turned, reached up, and caught the ball snugly. Asa, too, slowed down and stopped. He could hit okay, but he was small. Talent and technique could not create power.

TWO

WHEN THEY MOVED INTO THE BIG TWO-STORY HOUSE, Dave did not seem to want to let Asa have one of the two second-floor bedrooms to himself. The master bedroom, with its own bathroom, was on the first floor, in the rear of the house; the room that seemed logical for Asa was in the front of the second floor, over the living room. It was a nice room, with three dormer windows, a peaked ceiling, and a walk-in closet. Asa gravitated toward it as if he had been born there. But then, he was getting to be pretty quick about finding his spot in a new house: this was his tenth move and he was barely eleven.

On the day they moved in—the first time Asa saw the place—he raced up the stairs with the large box containing his comic-book collection, which he had carried on his lap from their old house. Dave grumbled, "Not so fast now," and Asa froze on the landing.

"What's the matter?" Asa's mother asked. Asa heard in her voice something warning, dangerous, tired.

Dave said, "Well, I don't know that the boy should have that room."

"And why not?"

For the first time Dave noticed the dangerous tone. He looked at her and frowned. "Well, it's a big room. An awfully nice room."

"Ah," she said, nodding. "*Too* nice, you mean. For him to just *get*."

"Well—"

"He should have to go through some hardship first, or something. Have to share it, maybe—the way you did, of course, with your two brothers." She made a show of looking around earnestly. "Trouble is, see, there are no other kids."

Dave cocked his head to the side and pushed his chin out a smidgeon, a sign that he was just about to be inclined to begin to get a little tough. "Now, be careful."

"And," said Asa's mother, "as for hardships— well, it's a bit late to come up with some task to make him earn the right to a room in our house, since we're moving in right now and all, but maybe we can think of something. What could we have him do? We don't want anything to be too *easy* for him, do we? Got to keep it *rugged*. Let's see—he could refinish the floors up there. We said they needed it. How about that?"

"Look—"

"No? Well, how about he slates the roof? Too

wet today. Besides, we really don't want it to be some simple one-time job, do we? To get yourself a nice room, you should have to go through something long and twisty. He's already done a divorce and a remarriage and seven moves in three years, so we can't let him repeat any of that. Just be going through the motions. Well hey, *I* know!"

She snapped her fingers. Dave just glared at her. Asa watched from the landing, stooping to see their faces under the ceiling. His mother took a step up to Dave and put a hand on his chest. She smiled. He scowled, unmoving.

"*I* know," she repeated. "If we can't think of anything to get out of him, well, then, we can just reserve the right to task him whenever we feel like it in the future!" She gave a fake gay laugh that made even Asa wince. But Dave took it without a flinch, right in his face. She went on, patting him on the chest fondly. "We can just give him a hard time every now and then on general principles, because he's got this nice room he doesn't really deserve. How about that? Solves a *lot* of our problems. Honey!" she called up the stairs to Asa. Her voice was strong now, natural and direct, without sarcasm. "Go ahead and pick your room and carry your stuff up and arrange it however you like. Leave room for your bed." Then she returned Dave's glare, took her hand slowly off his chest, and went out the door to get another load from the rented truck.

In the next couple of months Asa decided that what bothered Dave about his room was not so much that it was nice, but that it was far away: he could really be alone there. There were several things about this that could not fail to aggravate Dave, Asa knew. First, Dave did not trust the state of solitude. He clearly did not think anything good could come of someone being by himself; Asa could not speculate about exactly which evils Dave believed arose from such isolation, but it was obvious that bad things were supposed to happen when you let a kid think too much, or play by himself, or read. Second, Dave did not trust Asa. Again Asa was unable to come up with ideas of what specific sins he was capable of committing up there—but he knew it wasn't really a matter of specifics. Something about him made Dave suspicious.

So he was never all that surprised when Dave came quietly up the stairs and popped into the room without knocking. Asa *did* keep his door closed. Dave always asked him why—implying that anyone who shut his door must have something to hide—and Asa always replied that he liked being "snug." This was true. Also, Asa liked listening to rhythm and blues at low volume on his radio and did not want the music to intrude on the television shows Dave and his mother watched downstairs. These reasons never seemed quite to mollify Dave, who looked suspiciously around the room from a step or two inside the doorway. Asa was usually reading, or drawing, or building a model car, so after his snap check Dave always withdrew without explaining the visit by so much as a feigned message.

One Saturday morning in early October Asa was sitting on the floor in a dormer, reading *Treasure Island* beneath the window, when Dave opened the door and stepped in. Asa looked up. Something was different. Dave was wearing sneakers, thick-soled black hightops. Asa had never seen them before. Even stranger, Dave was holding a football in his right hand.

"It's sunny," he said. He snuck a quick look around the room, but he seemed to be trying to keep his eye on Asa this time.

"Yes," said Asa. He held up his book. "I'm reading by it."

Dave started to say something but stopped his mouth. Then, with an underhand snap of the wrist, he flicked the football across the room in a whirling spiral. Without thinking, Asa dropped *Treasure Island* and caught it.

Dave grinned. "Good," he said.

Asa stared at the ball gripped unmoving in his hands. He was amazed: A second ago it had been whizzing two ways at once. "How did you make it go like that?" he said.

"Come on out and I'll teach you," Dave said.

So they went out and threw the football to each other for almost three hours. During that time, Dave taught Asa quite a few very specific things— grip, arm motion, foot placement, the shifting of weight, the rotating of hips. How to plot a path for the throw to drop just where the running receiver would be. Dave did not instruct so much as show, perhaps—"Watch my wrist," he would say, (instead of an analytical explanation)—but Asa knew how to learn things.

He was thrilled by the whole day: the cool edge in the air, the dry detachment with which Dave offered simple expertise, the thin yellow of the light, and the passing itself, especially the eerie connection he felt between the hand that had just released the ball arcing into space and the hands that caught and carried it away on an unchecked run. But there was more going on than just the sport. After a half hour Asa realized quite clearly that for the first time he and Dave were giving free play to the natural tendencies that usually brought them into tight-lipped contention: Dave was being an authority, and Asa was being intelligent.

During their first couple of years as fake father and fake son, Dave had tried to make Asa do many things—but he was terrible at it, like a bulldog sergeant major crushing the recruit in a bad army movie. As for Asa, he tried to make Dave respect his ability to think—but he was a bit of a show-off, snapping out uncanny perceptions

about things he knew were supposed to be beyond his reach, racing ahead of both his mother
and Dave to note the end points of ramifications
just opening before them. When the family considered anything at all together, from dinner at a
particular restaurant to a drive in a rainstorm, Asa
rattled off the string of consequences attendant on
each alternative choice. At eleven he was already a
pedant. Dave, at thirty, was still a bully.

They both knew the terms of their life together.
But sports, it appeared, was different—perhaps it
was not really a part of life. Dave could show him
how to let a football slip off his fingertips without
the chippy force that usually pushed his com-
mands, and Asa could accept the instruction without feeling belittled, without having to show that
he had already figured it out alone. Asa asked
himself: Why? Was it because sports did not "matter" (the way saying "Sir" and "Ma'am" in exactly
the right tone of voice mattered, or having a short
enough haircut, or any of the other things that
Dave demanded)? Or was it because sports—
clearly a male domain—never brought Asa's
mother into play between them? Asa thought

about it a lot, as he and Dave expanded on this newfound opportunity to enjoy, if not harmony, at least cooperative neutrality, by playing football and then basketball throughout the fall and winter.

One day they were shooting foul shots and Dave missed five in a row. Without thinking (he *never* spoke to Dave without thinking; the slightest carelessness could be a step into a red elevator shaft of wrath) Asa said, "You're not bending your knees before you shoot. So you're standing up too straight and your shots are flat and long." He added, as if suddenly aware of his temerity, "Maybe we're tired."

Dave stared at him. His eyes narrowed for a moment. Then he looked at the basket, bent his knees, and bobbed a couple of times, spinning the ball in his hands as he eyed the rim. He hit three shots in a row, then said, "Let's go." On the way home he patted Asa once on the shoulder and said, "You're learning good." Asa *felt* good—cold, appraising, alert only to the technicalities of form and result: he was relieved of emotion. This was sports: action without emotion, liberty from putting anything on the line.

Or so it seemed, for a long time over the winter. Certainly there was less tension in the house, and Asa equated less tension with less emotion. He and Dave would return home at dusk, and his mother would be happily setting out the family dinner; they would eat quietly while she talked nonstop; Dave would take his second cup of coffee into the den to watch television, and Asa would scoot upstairs. Often he snuck back down a little later, after Dave had fallen asleep in front of *The Beverly Hillbillies* or *77 Sunset Strip*, to help his mother wash dishes. Oddly, this was a household job Dave had never assigned to him; Asa was certain it was because he did not like the idea of the two of them alone together.

One night as he was scrubbing a glass casserole dish, his mother said, "I'm sure glad to see my boys getting along so good."

He hesitated; when she expressed herself in this girlish-whimsy way, complete with grammatical mistakes—he couldn't convince himself she was being genuine. How could she be so shrewd and resolute sometimes, then so content with cuteness at others? He sensed a huge longing in his mother, a catalogue of keen needs that were beyond him and Dave, even together, even with his long-gone father thrown in for good measure. And often when he suspected her of playing a part, he sensed behind it a desperate will to sincerity; she was trying out a way of being someone people could readily understand. It was not the kind of acting he held in contempt. It was a sadder, nobler performance.

"We're kind of having fun," he said to his casserole dish.

His mother sighed happily and rubbed brisk circles into a dinner plate with her towel. "Fun," she said.

Asa tried to keep it going. He said, "Dave's teaching me a lot."

His mother said nothing for a moment, and he imagined she was putting the plate away. But then her arms closed around him from behind. "Maybe," she said, her mouth pressed against his ear. "Maybe so, baby doll. But 'fun,' now—well, I think my boy has just as much to teach *him*. And *that's* what I like."

One day in late March, he and Dave were walking along a cinder path that wound through woods to the basketball court outside his school. Buds were poised everywhere, as if waiting for a cue; a sweeping glance took in the sight of a misty green below the surface of everything, but focusing on a single branch showed nothing especially verdant. Asa drew a happy sigh and announced that he wanted to play Little League baseball.

Dave frowned. "Well," he said. "Not much of a game."

Asa was ready for this; perhaps the weather made him quick, even funny. "I think baseball's got everything," he said with a smile, "including dullness."

Dave grunted. They walked on. Around them the sumac was sending up its antennalike shoots. Dave said, "It's complicated, baseball. Too many things to do—catch, throw, swing a bat, run bases. Two months, you can barely shoot a jump shot. Too hard for you."

Asa amazed himself by laughing. "Hey, but you're a *great* teacher," he said, going so far as to clap Dave on the back. "And I'm a fantastic student."

There wasn't much Dave could say to that. So, reluctantly, he agreed. But from that moment, Asa felt their cool detachment begin to clench into some sort of grip. Starting the next day, they practiced baseball—not all those complicated parts of the game, but just the elemental art of hitting the ball. However, Dave's instruction lost its air of indifference, took on an edge; and Asa found himself more and more determined to show his stepfather something unexpected and strong. It was still spring, and in the paths and fields fern tendrils unwound and hot new leaves splayed outward. But he and Dave turned away from the green and tightened up.

THREE

SOMEHOW THE GREAT TABLE TALK TEAM COULD NOT score. In the fourth inning two men reached base with no one down, but the next two hitters struck out on terrible pitches, and the third lashed a line drive that Asa outran to right center and caught one-handed over his shoulder. In the fifth the Cool Guy on the mound walked the bases full, and as he came out of the game, his teammates looked at each other almost with relief: "Ah, *this* is more like it, *this* is where we lose." The next hitter chopped a grounder the new pitcher scooped at and missed—but his mitt knocked it back to home, where the catcher was waiting with his foot on the plate for the force-out. Feeling better, the pitcher threw hard down the pipe to the following batter, who hit the ball on the nose right back at him. It smacked into his glove, spinning him half around; the base runners thought he was watching the ball sail in a flash into center field, so they ran. Grinning, the pitcher trotted to first and tagged the base for the easiest of double plays.

As the innings passed, the facts began to sink in to the Cool Guys: they were not being clobbered. Hits started to fall in. In the top of the fifth they got three base runners, and only a pickoff and a double play kept them off the scoreboard. In the top of the sixth, the last inning, Tim led off with a sharp single to center. Asa, swinging down at a low pitch, crushed it into the infield. Spraying dirt, the ball bounded over the ducking second baseman, and Tim hustled to third. Freddie struck out trying to uppercut a sacrifice fly to the outfield, but everyone hollered happily from the dugout. Asa, on first, saw three of the Table Talk infielders glance fretfully at the hopeful Cool Guys jumping up and down. Then, he, too, knew Quik-E-Freeze had a chance.

Pete, the catcher, was up. Catchers, according to Coach Henderson, were supposed to be the smartest hitters, because they knew all the tricks a pitcher could call upon. Pete, failing to notice that at this level of baseball there were no tricks, believed him, and Asa could tell that for this at bat Pete thought himself cunning as a raccoon. He waggled his bat, cocked his head, relaxed his hands, and shot beams of daring at the pitcher. It was unnerving, apparently: the first two pitches scudded in the dirt. Pete didn't even watch them.

As he leaned into his lead at first base, Asa thought: How could this be? How could we all know what is about to happen? For it was clear that everyone did know. The Table Talk bench, usually as cute and mechanical in its cheering as a Baptist child choir on TV, now slunk forward in gloomy foreboding. The fielders, brows wrinkled, kicked at pebbles between pitches, sometimes not looking up until the ball was on the way to the plate. The pitcher sucked in breaths as if they were cough syrup. But the Cool Guys—hey, life was great! Tim stood on third with his hand on his hips and blew a large pink bubble that did not pop. Asa's legs tingled with speed-to-be. The boys in the dugout laughed. It was as if Pete had already hit the ball somewhere far away. There was no doubt.

The pitcher decided it was time to get it over with. He threw an easy pitch that floated to the plate at the level of the FREEZE! logo on Pete's chest, and Pete stepped and swung. The ball was in the sky before anyone heard the solid *tock* of impact. Asa held back, waiting to see it land, but Tim streaked home and hit the plate at the same instant the ball dropped onto the grass way beyond the running boys in left center. Now Asa swept around second and burned toward third. The "coach" there—a third-string infielder—was too busy cheering with two hands in the air, his eyes on the ball, to give Asa a sign to stop or go, so Asa cut across the base and sped on toward home. As he bore down on the catcher, his universe shrank: he was running in a tunnel and the opening at the end got smaller as he got nearer. There, the last thing in the world, was the All-Star catcher, his mask off, his face sweaty and red, crouched with his weight on both legs, blocking the plate; his eyes flashed over Asa's head, pleading for the ball; his mitt, as Asa watched, began to turn and reach. Asa slid without slackening his speed, shooting his right foot between the catcher's legs at the plate and kicking out with his left at one of the boy's planted legs. He scooted almost entirely through before the catcher fell heavily onto him. Beneath his left hip he felt the hard rubber of the plate.

The umpire above him yelled something, but Asa did not pay attention. He was too busy trying to untangle himself from James Neal and stand up; now, finally, it seemed to be his turn to hoot and holler and leap about, and he wanted to strike while the urge was on—deep in his chest he was ready to be delivered of the strange, cool restraint that always kept him apart from his teammates' ups and downs. Up at last, he shook free and spun toward the dugout with a wordless whoop, a scream of joy, waving his fists in front of him as if he had caught something wild in each. But his teammates stood with their mouths open, watching someone large who was at that moment bustling past Asa toward home plate, making noise. Asa, after a glance at the stunned boys, turned to follow their stare.

What had rushed past him was Coach Henderson. It was hard to recognize him. The crisply mannered, fine-featured man was now hunched and flailing, his face like a plum-colored knot squeezed out from his humpy shoulders. He was snarling at the umpire; Asa noticed, as the ump stepped away and Coach Henderson turned his head to follow, that the coach had crooked teeth. Asa had never seen them before; he would never have expected them to be crooked. The opposing coach, a consistently jolly Greek man named Stravros who owned the Table Talk Bakery, was out of his dugout, trying to catch Coach Henderson by one of his elbows. There seemed to be four or five of them in the air, but he couldn't snag one. Then the umpire, his face full of fear, shot his arm into the air.

Still Asa did not know; he stood there not knowing, his fists of celebration still made. It was only when Coach Henderson stormed by, flushed with anger and, now, with what Asa recognized as shame, and said, "Sorry, Asa, but you were safe, my boy," that he realized. He was not safe. He was out. The umpire had called him out.

He walked back to the dugout. A couple of boys patted him and said, "We got one anyhow." On the field, as if in a hurry to reestablish the nature of things, a Cool Guy swung at a bad pitch and popped out. Asa found his glove and trotted out to center.

Out? Well, perhaps. How did he know? He hadn't been watching: he had been *in* there, inside the moment—tangled in legs and red shin guards and twisting arms at the end of the tunnel, not watching, not thinking, just concentrating on getting to the plate. What kind of judge was he? For once, it was up to somebody else to see the sequence of things, and somebody had done so. Out? It could be. There were only two choices, and one had been made. Asa would have preferred being safe, but preference was not knowledge. He wasn't angry. In a way, he was thrilled, simply to have been too involved to know.

The Table Talk batter swung at the first pitch and lofted a long fly to left. Asa watched without surprise as it soared, peaked, kept flying, and cleared the fence by twenty feet. The Baptist child choir woke up. He did not watch the hitter jump and dance as he ran the bases; they all did that, and he hated it. If *he* ever hit a home run, he would put his head down and scurry. He supposed he would be proud, but pride was private. Eventually the gamboling Table Talk boy touched home, and the game was tied.

Next up, the pitcher cracked a line drive that hit the shortstop in the chest. The Cool Guy collapsed, cringing and crying, while the ball spun like a planet in the dirt. He came out of the game, replaced by the kid who had been coaching third base when Asa had run around it. The runner was held at first. The next batter popped up a bunt. Pete snatched it out of the air and nearly doubled the runner off first. One away. Left-handed hitter. He swung at the first pitch and bounced it on one hop over the right-field fence. Men on second and third. One out.

The next Table Talk hitter knocked a grounder that Tim dove to his left to spear. Springing up, he drew back his arm at the runner who had taken off from third, until the boy dove back. Then Tim hummed a throw across to first and beat the runner by a stride. It was a great play. Asa hollered Tim's name. *Great* play. Two out. They could get out of this. If they did not let up, they could get out of it.

James Neal sauntered to the plate. He was a right-handed hitter but his power was to center. He was the best hitter in their league: every swing was level and true, no matter what the pitch, a disciplined slash that swept the ball through the infield in a blink. When James hit home runs—and Asa could think of half a dozen he had seen—they were line drives that just kept rising as they flew. Once he had struck one over Asa's head into the tin scoreboard, and its impact had sprung five numbers off their nails onto Asa's grass.

Asa looked around at his teammates. They were watching James Neal advance to the batter's box, and they were all slinking. *No!* Asa wanted to holler. *Stop! We can do this guy! There are two out! Just one out to get and we are back at bat and we can win it.* He wanted them to see this—it was so simple! Asa kicked at the grass. They were giving up. He did not understand giving up—that was all. Giving up did not *work*.

The first pitch whizzed in. James Neal took a cut and everybody gasped. Asa leaped a step forward, but it was a foul back up over the Quik-E-Freeze dugout into the night. The runners, cocky in their trots, touched up, and waited; with two out they would fly on any hit. Both would score on a single. James Neal waved his bat and stared at the pitcher. He was a very emotional player, but there was no feeling in his face right now, only concentration. And here came the pitch.

Asa realized as soon as James Neal started his swing that he ought to have been playing in closer. So he started his run just as the ball sprang off the bat dead on a line four feet above second base. Asa did not slow down; he sprinted from his jump start, straight at where the ball was dipping, dipping, touching the wet grass, and rising in a long, low bounce right at him. Somewhere in his awareness he registered the whirling arms of the base runners romping safely home, the yowls from the Table Talk dugout, the cheers of half the parents springing to their feet in the stands. But mostly he was aware of three things—the ball he was speeding to intercept, the moon face of his first baseman turned this way to watch the hit, and James Neal, his grin bright with the grandest pleasure, his arms held straight up, his legs scissoring as he celebrated with a couple of leaps on his way to first. Somewhere inside Asa there was a whiz of physics that added these things up, and though he hadn't time to feel it, he knew there would be happiness in a moment. For now, he gloved the ball and plucked it out with his throwing hand and planted his left foot perfectly, then with every ounce of momentum developed over fifty feet of sprint he whipped his hips and snapped his arm and spun into a follow-through.

He watched the ball. It flickered through the air and smacked into the barely opened mitt of the first baseman while James Neal was coming down from his last scissor leap, six feet from first.

The first baseman stared into his mitt at the ball, then looked down at his foot on the bag. Nobody cheered. James Neal stopped, gaped, then shook his head and looked around. He walked to first and stomped on it. "It's a clean *single*," he said to no one, his voice winding up for tears.

The Cool Guy infielders still didn't get it; neither did most of the boys on the Table Talk bench. But they all began to see that Asa got it. He trotted in with his head down, and one by one the players grew still and watched him. His rubber spikes crunched on the infield dirt. No one spoke but James Neal; he ran to the umpire, who stood between first and second, watching Asa approach.

"It's a clean *single*," he pleaded. His cheeks were red as match heads. He grabbed the umpire by the left arm but the ump shook him off without looking at him. Then, slowly, the man raised his right arm until his fist poised high above his ear, as if he had a knife. He watched Asa; only James Neal did not.

As Asa crunched by, he glanced up and met the umpire's look. "Out," said the man clearly.

FOUR

AFTER A COUPLE OF WEEKS ON A LOW TWILIT FIELD not far from their house, Asa found he and Dave were communicating entirely through the baseball itself. At first there were a few blunt instructions, but it became clear that not only did Dave dislike baseball—he also did not know it very well. After telling Asa he should "watch the ball" and "not try to kill it" he hadn't much to add that Asa couldn't pick up better simply by swinging. So Dave pitched, hard, from a bag of old baseballs he had wangled from a semipro team sponsored by the company he worked for. Asa stood and swung and stood and swung and stood and swung.

It also became clear that the absence of words did not mean they had nothing to say. Between them, suddenly, the air crackled with danger; through that air passed the ball. Asa could feel shoves of anger or doubt or pure competitiveness in the spin and speed of the pitch at the moment he struck it—always as hard as he could—with his bat. He was certain his replies were just as clear: high-strung line drives, overmatched popups, meek ground balls, and spirited, sloping flies he watched with a burning in his chest that could not have been more violent and celebratory if he had strode out to Dave and socked him. Two hours might pass without a word, but at the end they would both be drained.

It was not fun, but it was practice. And it worked: pitch by pitch Asa learned things, and soon he was becoming a hitter. Occasionally he sensed some grudging satisfaction in Dave when he lashed out six or seven tough pitches in a row to all parts of the field; they both seemed to re-member, if only for the moment, that Asa's progress meant they were *both* doing well.

But sometimes they forgot. If Asa hit too many pitches too hard, Dave would hum one way inside at him, and Asa would have to spin away from it into the dirt. The first time this happened, he said, "Hey!" and Dave said, "Hey what? Part of the game," and motioned for him to stand back in; the next pitch was right over the plate. After that Asa said nothing. He saved his energy to bash the next ball.

One day, Asa stroked a long fly to dead center and stood watching it contentedly, holding a hand up to Dave as a signal that he should wait until Asa finished gloating. The ball landed far out in the green; Asa sighed happily. When he lowered his hand, Dave hit him with the ball. There was no pretense about it. He did not even wind up the way he did for a pitch: he let Asa step up to the plate and then he drew his arm back and threw—hard, always hard—directly at the boy's ribs. Asa froze. The ball seemed to take forever to arrive, but then it sprang at him and burrowed into his bones. He dropped backward and landed flat, screaming and rolling over and over. He knew he was crying because he felt mud on his cheeks from tears and dust, but he did not hear a thing, nor did he notice any vision: the whole world was a hole in his side. But before he could think, the pain switched over, and the world became a fury in his heart. He stood up.

Dave was out in the outfield collecting the balls Asa had hit, putting them in the canvas bag. His back was turned, and Asa knew he would keep it turned. Asa looked around home plate. There were three balls he had fouled into the backstop. He picked up his bat and one of the balls. In left center, Dave bent, straightened, bent, and straightened. Asa tossed his ball and hit it viciously. It sailed toward Dave with good distance, but tailed away toward right; Asa watched as it whizzed over Dave's head and landed twenty feet beyond him. Dave looked up and watched it land, too, but he did not turn around. In fact, he remained upright and motionless, as if offering his back in case Asa wanted to hit another. Asa did not. He left the other two balls and took his bat home.

The family ate dinner as usual that night—or almost as usual. It was obvious that something had happened, but neither Dave nor Asa spoke of it. Asa saw his mother studying Dave, and knew she was studying him when he wasn't looking. He wondered if Dave would tell; he certainly wouldn't.

The next day he remained in his room after school, reading comics. As the hour for their daily practice approached, he reached for more comic books; there was no question about whether or not the workouts would continue. They were finished.

But about ten minutes past the time, someone knocked on his door. He said, "What?" and the door opened. His mother stepped in.

She was wearing white tennis shoes and one of Dave's golf caps and holding Asa's bat in her right hand. His glove hung over her left wrist: she wore it like a bracelet. He stared. She smiled. "Let's go," she said.

"But—"

"Come on. Your tryout is in two weeks. Let's go chuck a few."

He started to protest. But in her eyes was a look that made him rise. It was part command, part entreaty; part confidence, part loss. He went with her.

On their way to the field she did not say anything to explain why she was taking Dave's place;

instead, she pointed out weeds that were coming into flower or trees that had brought forth buds. Asa nodded and commented politely, softly. In his life there had been half a dozen times when the air around him filled with an aching sweetness, a thick feeling of fragile bliss that poured into him and out of him at once, and moved with him as he moved. Always it was sad as well as happy, and always it ended suddenly. It came when someone gave him something and he took it without knowing. When the feeling was gone, sometimes the gift was too. He did not know, as he walked to the park beside his chatty mother, whether what she gave would last for him or not, but the swelling of sweetness and woe clouded around them, and he drew it in all the way to the pitcher's mound. By the time he explained why this strange little hill was here and showed her how to put on his glove, the cloud had vanished.

Her first pitch was six feet outside and ten feet high. Her second was lower, but farther away. Her third arrived near the plate on second bounce, and he gave it a tap into right field. "See," she yelled, gleefully. "Hooray for us!"

They had brought only the one ball. Asa re-trieved it. When he came back, he went to the mound.

"Know what?" he said. "I've really pretty much done nothing but bat up to now, for two weeks."

She looked at him warily, unwilling to be pa-tronized. "So?"

He tried to sound chipper and spontaneous. "What I need is the chance to field a lot."

"Field?" She looked around. "A lot?"

"Sorry—it means to catch the ball, make throws: play defense. I, um, only got the chance to do offense before. There didn't seem to be much interest in the other side. But it's just as important. At the tryouts they watch you hit, but they also make you catch and throw. It's actually more com-plicated than swinging the bat."

She thought, liked it, nodded. "Okay." She smiled. "I'm your defensive coach. What do I do?"

He had a feeling she could be taught to toss the ball up and hit grounders to him, certainly more easily than she could be taught to pitch. He was right. In a few minutes she had learned to toss it, grip the bat, wait for the ball to come down, and chop at it with a short stroke. He moved out to the shortstop spot, and for almost an hour she pounded it at him, slow, high-bouncing balls sprayed all over the infield. It was actually wonderful: after a dozen grounders he was breathless and sweaty and fully stretched. It was plainly wonderful for his mother, too, though she had apparently decided to play it cool. She was all business as she hit the ball, dropped the bat, crouched with her hands apart in front of her, and clapped them over the soft rollers he sent back to her after making his catch. There was no more "Hooray!" and self-celebration: she made it clear this was a natural thing now, no big deal. Nevertheless, it was just as clear they were supposed to be having fun and they were. The next day he did not wait for her to come to his room; he got the equipment and stood at her bedroom door while she tied her sneakers.

Within a few days she was able to pop little line drives at him. From there she moved easily into short fly balls. Before long, he was getting all the defensive work he could wish for. She had a good instinct for mixing up her hits, moving him around, making him go back to his left and then drawing him into a charge to his right. Her grounders got trickier; she could smash them on a lower trajectory now, or squib them with English so they trickled away from him if he got lazy and waited on one knee instead of running forward. The better she got, the less serious she pretended to be; the more she yanked him around, the more she chattered and laughed. He laughed too, even, sometimes, in the middle of a lunging catch that required all his reach and concentration. Every ball she hit had wit behind it. He got the joke as he made the play.

The tryouts approached; soon they arrived at the Friday before the Sunday when he would report, alone, to the municipal park at eight in the morning. Two more days! He was excited; he leaned toward the date with confidence that his chance to show something unexpected was at hand. Two days! Still, he tried to focus on the remaining practices. His workouts with his mother had gotten longer, so the two of them took breaks in the middle and sat for ten minutes by a creek that ran along one side of the field. On this Friday the weather was hot. Before sitting, he took off his shirt.

Squinting at the water, he saw his mother stare at him, look away, then stare again. He looked at her. Her eyes were on his torso. He looked down. There, in the ribs beneath his left arm, was the baseball-sized bruise he had carried for two weeks. It was an old bruise by now, greenish and blotchy, with one weird feature: the raised stitches of the ball had left two perfect curved marks of a deeper bruise, exact in their replication of the tiny bird-feet pattern, purple and geometric. The mark held no horror for Asa; indeed, he had quickly come to regard it as a fascinating study in the quirkiness of skin tissue, noting each change in color and texture. He checked it coolly each morning, then forgot about it. Following his mother's eyes now, he realized it was an ugly thing. He pretended to shiver, said, "Actually, it's a little breezy," and put his shirt back on.

His mother was looking him in the eye now. He did not know what to say, so he shrugged. She did not let him off with that. He said, "No big deal, you know?"

"Oh sure," she said. "Of course not." She held his eyes for a moment longer; he had to say something, so he said, "It's, like, just something guys don't mind." He grinned, gave himself a smack right on the bruise. She winced but he didn't. "See?" he said. "Doesn't hurt." He chuckled, shook his head, smiled at the creek. In his peripheral vision he saw her continue to stare at him. It was unnerving. So, without really intending to, he began to talk. He had thought he might just say a couple of reassuring things about his relationship with Dave, but before he knew it, he had drifted into deeper waters. He found himself defending his stepfather rather cleverly, though his mother had not charged him with anything. It must be *very* difficult being a stepfather, he said; especially if you married the woman you had loved long ago and now here she was at last—but this time she had a *kid* with her! Asa joked about the terrible inconvenience of this—how the kid must get in the way, change everything; he did a cute job of imitating the frustration of the adults. He chuckled at his own wit; his mother looked at the creek.

As he listened to himself chatter, Asa knew he

was not pleading a trumped-up defense of Dave just to soothe his mother's anguish. He was pleading because he knew that despite Dave's roughness, the man was mostly trying to do strong, decent, difficult things with his stepson and his wife. Especially his wife. Asa was aware that *he* was not the main challenge in Dave's life. He had witnessed this marriage for years now. His head whirled sometimes with a sense of the history of these two people, fading back into the past, beyond his conscious understanding. But he did understand a great deal, really; at certain moments he knew he was in the presence of something big. It was true that much of the time this big, sweet force couldn't be easily perceived beneath the shadows of Dave's tyranny and his mother's torment. But sometimes it did shine, even from Dave. Asa had watched Dave coax her, without a trace of impatience, out of several of the fits of despair to which she so often seemed doomed—fits that, left unchecked, took over her life in a matter of hours. Twice in the previous year she had spun so quickly into her own darkness that Dave had handed her over to the state hospital at Butner, for nearly a month each time. Coaxing her out early was work that required a strength and self-assurance Asa knew he could not approach—but he could readily admire it in Dave. At other times he had watched Dave gently, teasingly build long, slow jokes from sly references to this and that old business from their life, as they drove along in the car for hours—jokes that accumulated power as they tickled deeper and deeper, drawing her up through perfectly paced stages of amusement and laughter until she reached a reckless, weeping hilarity that left her spread-eagled over the car seat shaking, sniffling, wailing. During these crescendos Dave simply watched the road and smiled.

So now, filled with this urgent sympathy, Asa went on babbling to his mom about how difficult being a stepfather must be. And it wasn't just difficult being a stepfather in general. It must be *really* tough being *his* stepfather—Asa's. He was, he knew, a very weird kid. He said this lightly, with a wry shake of the head and a rueful smile, *Oh, that Asa*. It was an expression he had often inspired—with a less kindly humor to it—in his stepfather.

His mother surprised him by wheeling around

in a sudden fury. "What is this?" she sputtered. "What is supposed to be so weird about *you,* Asa?"

Her flare burned off his pretense of lightheartedness. But he had started something, so he plugged on, without playacting now. "Well," he said, "you know. I'm—*different.* I mean—here we are in the South and Dave has this big family and all the kids are normal Southern kids. They go to church all the time, they take it very easy, they don't worry about much. *Great* sense of humor—tease a lot, but it's because they like you, you know. That's the way Dave was when he was a kid, I know, and that's the way he *likes* kids. That's what kids *are,* to him. But I'm different. I care too much about things they don't even notice. Stupid things I know don't really matter, really. Like, I mind that they crease my comic books. When they come over, they come in, all friendly, and I really like them, I like my cousins—I wish *I* was that friendly all the time—and they plop down and yank out a bunch of my comics. That's okay. I can put them back in order. But they *fold* them, fold the covers back, sometimes they wad them up and put them in their back pockets to go down and eat. It's dumb to care so much about it, I know, but—I try to keep them kind of neat. I take care of them, is all. But I know it doesn't matter. What matters is that we are all cousins, we are all family. You're not supposed to let junk like that—like stupid comic books—come in the way of your love of your family. But I can't help it—before the love comes on, I start worrying about my comics, and I hate doing it, and Dave is right."

"Right? What does he say that is right?"

Asa had not planned on this, but now he was nervous and upset and he couldn't seem to stop. He tried to back off. "Oh, nothing. I mean, he's *right*. He's just trying to help me."

"What does he say?"

"He lets me know I'm being sort of a nervous finicky guy. Like maybe I like *things* better than *people*, you know? And that's wrong, I know it is. So I ought to be different. It *is* better to be kind of loose and easy about stuff."

"Oh yes," she said. "Like Dave. He's very loose and easy about stuff, isn't he? That's probably how you got that bruise."

Asa shut up and plucked grass. His mother watched him for a minute, then stared back out across the creek. He snuck a look at her; she wasn't crying or anything, at least. After a few minutes he asked if they could resume their practice.

She was grave for the rest of their workout. On the way home, silence waited between them. Then she said, "I'm very sorry, Asa."

He pretended not to know what she was talking about. A few minutes later she added, "It's no good."

"No, don't," he said. He had to say *something*. "It's fine." He gave her a pretty good smile. Then he took her hand, and they held hands all the way home.

In the middle of the night he woke up to find Dave shaking him. He smelled coffee, but it was too dark for morning and he could feel he hadn't been asleep long enough.

"Wake up," said Dave. "I need your help. We have to get some coffee in her." Then he ran from the room. Asa pushed his covers away and followed him downstairs.

Dave, in pajama bottoms, was in the kitchen pouring coffee into a mug. "Too hot," he said. "Ice." He yanked open the freezer and pulled out an ice tray and smacked it very hard against the edge of the counter. Chips of ice sprayed all over. He picked a few off the counter and put them in the coffee, then said, "Come on," and walked past Asa, leaving the freezer door open.

They went into the bedroom. The light was on. His mother lay diagonally across their bed, her arms at her sides; to Asa she looked strangely heavy and still, like a slab of wet clay. His throat went cold. "Is she—"

"She's—asleep," said Dave, giving him a quick look. He was on the far side of the bed, at her head. "Come here. We've got to get some coffee in her." He was flustered; it gave him an odd gentleness. "Do you want to hold her head or pour?"

"I'll hold her head." Asa went around and lifted his mother behind the neck. Dave held the mug up to her mouth and poured some coffee in. A little ran out of the corners of her mouth onto the sheets; the rest seemed to vanish until she coughed and spewed it.

"More," said Dave. This time her throat executed a kind of swallow.

Asa's arms were trembling; he was glad, actually. He knew he was in the middle of something that ought to be making him frantic, and instead he felt all cool and easy. The trembling showed he felt *something*, he guessed. "Why is she so asleep?" he asked.

Most of the coffee was in. Dave looked down into her throat, frowning. "Okay," he said. "Lie her back down."

Asa resisted the temptation to correct Dave's *lie* to *lay*; instead he said, "Maybe we should sit her up."

Dave looked at him. "Right," he said. He jammed pillows against the headboard of the bed, and they pushed her against them. Her head fell forward, and Dave pushed it back until the pillows held it up. Her head didn't seem to care. She was out. The only thing about her that moved was her lower lip, which pulled in a bit whenever she sucked a raggedy breath.

"Why is she so asleep?" Asa asked again.

Dave ran his fingers through his hair. "You

want some coffee too? I got to have some too."

Asa followed him into the kitchen. "If you don't tell me, I'm calling an ambulance," he said.

Dave was pouring coffee into the same mug. He turned as he poured. "No," he said, far more reasonably than Asa expected. "I mean, we don't need the ambulance. She's all right. Really. Just sleepy." He slurped some of the coffee and winced at the heat.

"Why is she so sleepy? Why do we have to wake her?"

Dave watched him over the edge of the mug as he took another, longer swallow. "Well, Sport," he said, with a tone almost cheery, "she kind of goofed. She had a headache, and she went into the bathroom in the middle of the night, and she took what she thought was an aspirin. But it was a sleeping pill. They look the same." He shrugged and lifted the mug.

"One sleeping pill?" Asa said.

Dave paused and considered, the mug an inch from his mouth. "Two," he said, and drank.

Asa went back into his mother's room. She had slumped sideways. The friction of the skin of her left cheek against the wooden headboard was all that held her up from lying down again; the pressure pulled her lip up above her gum on that side and opened her left eye. Asa looked at the eye. Nothing but white was showing.

He straightened her, and went into the bathroom. In the medicine cabinet there was nothing but shaving stuff and toothpaste. He looked under the sink. The wastebasket was on its side and a few wads of tissue lay near it. There was a brown prescription bottle upright on the floor there. Asa picked it up and read the name of the medicine: Seconal. Inside he found a single red, oval pill. There was no aspirin or aspirin bottle anywhere.

He went back into the bedroom. Dave was there, leaning close to her, watching for some sign; from his face it was obvious he had no clue about what he was waiting for. Asa said, "I'm calling the hospital."

"No!" Dave roared, spinning on him. The gentility was gone. "You will do nothing but what I say, you hear? This isn't a time for a kid to interfere, I don't care how smart he thinks he is."

He glared at Asa; the boy held his eye for a moment, then started to walk toward the kitchen. Dave said, "Wait," more gently, and came over to him.

"Listen, please," he said. *Please* was not a word Asa heard from him often; he listened.

Dave put his hands on Asa's shoulders and looked straight into his face. "Listen, son. That's my wife over there. Your mother, and my wife. We want her to wake up and be okay. Both of us. I would not let her sit there in danger, understand?"

"You lied about the pills," said Asa. "I can't trust you."

Dave groaned in exasperation, and with an offhanded force that seemed weary, almost casual, he thrust Asa straight back until the boy slammed into the side of a bureau. Asa's ears filled with a buzzing from the back of his head, but he stayed erect; Dave stepped close and squatted, sticking his face close.

"You'll pardon me for not giving a dingle," he said, "but right now I just don't feel all torn up with the need for your 'trust.' It's not something your mother's pining for over there, either.

Frankly, boy, I don't think you're the kind of person who will ever trust *anybody*. It kind of takes an honest heart to do that, you understand what I mean?"

"Yes," said Asa, "I do." Then with a concentration of all his strength he snapped his arm out and punched Dave flush on the temple. The shock of it felt good; he left his arm, stiff and solid, in the air between them as Dave jerked backward and sat down hard. Dave shook his head and blinked fast for a moment, but quickly his eyes found Asa's and they stared at each other. For some time neither spoke or looked away. Then Asa lowered his fist, and Dave smiled grimly. There was a red circle near his left eye.

"Well," he said. His voice gurgled a little; he cleared his throat. "Well. Now, I guess, we're even." He started to stand up, careful to lean away from Asa as he did so.

"We'll never be even," said Asa. "We shouldn't try."

Dave hesitated, then chuckled darkly and shook his head. He stood all the way up, stepped past Asa, and went to bend over Asa's mother.

Asa walked to the other side of the room and sat on the floor with his back against the wall.

Dave left after a few minutes. Asa remained, watching her. From time to time Dave checked in, bringing coffee, which he got down her without Asa's assistance. In a couple of hours her breathing got a little easier, but she showed no signs of waking up. At one point Asa went over and tried to hold her hand, but he felt stupid. So he sat on the floor and waited, and after a while he fell asleep.

He woke to the sound of heavy footsteps and Dave's voice cursing. He opened his eyes. The light was off and the room was pretty dark, but it was dawn beyond the curtained windows; a long shape was just falling forward onto the bed with a thick *WHUMP*. The bathroom light went on and Asa heard Dave curse again. He stood up and went to the door.

Dave was looking into the sink. It was full of jagged pieces of glass, some of them covered with amber goo. Thinking back, Asa realized that before the footsteps he had heard—and incorporated into his dream, something about a science class—

the sound of glass breaking. It was probably what had brought him to the surface. Glass breaking, heavy footsteps, his mother collapsing onto the bed, Dave cursing—he tried to put it together.

Dave turned. "She wanted to wash her hair," he said. But he spoke with a pitiful lack of conviction, and a moment later he added, in a low, defeated voice: "Get dressed, son."

They carried her out to the car in the faint blue light, and stretched her out in the backseat on some blankets. She seemed to be as heavily asleep as ever; Asa wondered how she could have waked up and gotten to and from the bathroom and then slipped back. But he didn't need to understand: there she was. They climbed into the front seat.

Dave took turns that led them out of town, onto the road that went north. Asa had not really expected they would go only to the hospital in town; things seemed too big for town, all of a sudden. "Excuse me," he said. "Are we going to Raleigh?"

Headlights flashed over Dave's face. "Yes we are."

He offered no explanation. But then Asa and his

mother never needed an explanation when they were taken to Raleigh: It was Dave's hometown, where all his family lived, and it drew them whenever they did not have a good reason to stay where they lived. He remembered suddenly that it was his mother's hometown too; this was a fact, but not one that he felt very keenly. For one thing, he had known her first in Washington; for another, they always spent all their time in Raleigh with Dave's family. She seemed as much of an outsider with them as Asa did, despite her native ability to talk the talk and mimic the behavior of the Southern wives who had never left.

"Is Mom going to Butner?" Asa said.

"Yes," Dave said. "She is."

Asa waited a long time to ask his next question. He waited while they rode between tobacco fields and past gas stations opening up for the day, while the sun rose, pink and then yellow and then white in a white sky. He listened for his mother's breathing over the rumble of the car, and every so often he heard a snaggled intake of air. Dave stopped for takeout coffee at a diner an hour up the road and bought Asa a honey bun. Asa waited until he had eaten his bun and Dave had drunk his coffee. He waited a while longer. Then, trying to sound very light, trying to sound as if it did not really matter a bit, he was just wondering, no problem at all, he asked: "Will we spend the night?"

Dave looked at him as if he must be nuts. "Of course," he said. He shook his head at the boy's strangeness, and Asa knew just what he was thinking. Imagine going to Raleigh and not spending the weekend!

Asa said nothing; he vowed he would not. But Dave surprised him. After only five minutes, he said, "Oh!" and hit the steering wheel with the palm of his right hand. He turned and looked at Asa.

"I'm sorry," he said. "You were supposed to try out for Little League tomorrow morning."

"It's all right," Asa said, looking straight ahead.

Dave hit the steering wheel another, harder lick, and cursed. And suddenly Asa could feel clearly that Dave's anger was curling toward the woman in the backseat. It was *her* fault. She had *done* this, deprived his stepson of a chance to be a regular boy. Asa had seen how Dave's shifty anger could work, and he knew that soon his missed tryout—indeed, perhaps the entirety of his strange life, all predicated upon this lost shot at normalcy—would be another black mark against her, another sin.

Well, for this Asa would not stand. If *he* could get by without anger, what right did Dave have to be mad? Whose tryout was it, anyway? So, looking over, Asa said firmly, "Oh, no. It's all right. I wasn't going to try out."

Dave frowned. "You weren't?"

"No," said Asa.

"Why not?"

Asa took a breath. Outside, a sparrow hawk fluttered in the wind over a red clay field. "Well," he said, "it's a complicated game."

Dave thought for a moment. Then he let out a long breath. "Well," he said, "I told you so."

"Yes," said Asa, "you did." And that seemed to do it. They spoke no more. Asa turned then to watch out the side window, in which he could see a reflection of his face, watching. The drive went on in silence. After a couple of hours, as he stretched, he decided the scrub shortstop, the one who had come in after the line drive popped the other boy in the chest—he decided this kid would hit a home run in the top of the eighth. Yes, he liked that. Quik-E-Freeze would win. He felt a little guilty about this, a little selfish. But what the heck, he would do it: the Cool Guys would win, and he would feel great. Somehow, he hoped, he deserved this.

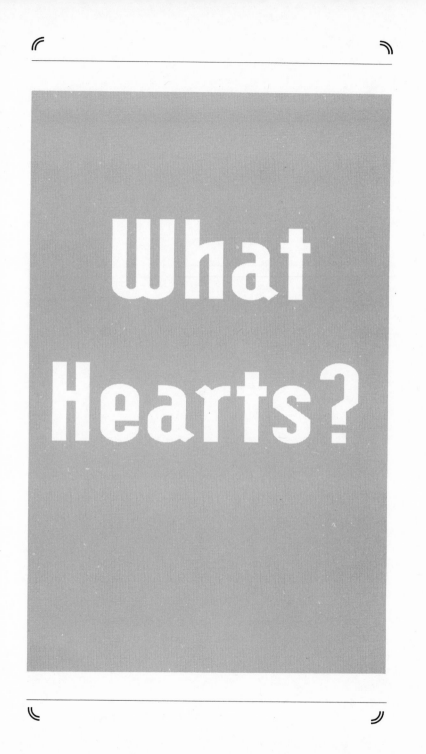

O N E

ASA WAS IN LOVE. HE LOVED JEAN WILLIAMS. SHE had been in his class since the fifth grade—or rather, he had been in hers. Fifth, sixth, and now seventh: Asa and his mother had not moved, and not moved, and not moved again. Now he could let himself count on seeing Jean every day—every moment, if he liked: a glance across the room would produce her. So far, everything he noticed about her was just right, whether it was the lean tension in her hands as she held a book, the sound of her voice pretending to order *"riz, petit pois"* from a mock restaurant in French class, or the curves of her neck when her hair swayed during field hockey games he watched after school in secret. It all added up to a sum inside him, a simple sum.

Their first meeting had been simple, too. One day midway through the fifth grade she came over during art class and sat sideways in the desk in front of him. Around them kids were gabbing: the art teacher allowed roaming and talking, in the spirit of creative freedom. Jean sat, turned toward him, and leaned one elbow on the edge of his desk. That small gesture, the intrusion into his territory, shook him with a sudden pleasure. It was powerful, and despite the ease with which she placed her elbow, Asa had a sense she knew how daring it was.

She said, "You have moved a lot, haven't you?"

Asa swallowed. He rarely answered a question without having figured out quickly what thought was behind it and what response was anticipated. This time he didn't have a clue. So he simply said, "Yes."

Jean nodded. Her eyes were technically brown, but when she got this close Asa could see they were a lot lighter than could possibly be imagined from a distance, nearer the color of butterscotch. She said, "I figured you had."

"How?" he asked.

"You work hard," she said. She leaned her chin lightly on the hand connected to the arm that rested on his desk. His legs tickled. She went on. "You figure things out, and you attack."

"Attack?" He must have looked horrified, for she laughed and blushed and put out her hand to tap him on the shoulder. *Tap, tap.* It was like the first time he had been touched by the ocean.

"I don't mean, like, to do battle," she said. "I mean—well, you seem to know how to *get* to people. What I like is, you seem to do it to be *nice*. And, well—" She looked at him, and with a thrill he saw that she too felt something that made her nervous. "And that's, well—*nice*." She laughed at her own verbal awkwardness, and got up.

That was it. From that point on, Asa had isolated Jean and his feelings about her from the rest of the world. This love—he started calling it that after a while—was his only known instance of simplicity. He wanted to protect it from the usual analysis and calculation that he cast over everything else out there. The protection worked. Things stayed simple. He and Jean became friends. They sometimes talked, mostly about school. They sometimes walked together, if they were going to the same place. Nothing in his behavior could be taken as a sign of the deepness inside him. He never meant to tell her anything about it. Except for wanting, at times, to reach out and touch her on the hand, lightly, very lightly, with a finger, he never meant to do anything direct.

But then, as the beginning of seventh grade approached, an ambition began to grow around the love: somehow, he wanted his feelings to emerge, to be strong in the light of day. He wanted them to do some work in the world. Hiding this fine stuff inside struck him as finicky, almost dishonest. *Stand up!* he felt like saying to himself; *Declare something*—to Jean, he supposed.

But he was wary of this newfound boldness. Several times he almost spoke to her—when he found himself next to her in the cafeteria line, or saw her alone in a library aisle, looking at the mysteries—but he stopped short. He was not nervous. He just had the nagging feeling that he lacked some kind of knowledge, not about himself or Jean, but about loving.

Willing for the first time to learn, he realized that he was—had long been—surrounded by public examples of the things lovers did. For two years he had seen the same billboard beside the public library, bearing a gaudy photo of a young man twirling a young woman in some kind of dance performed in a wooded dell, with hot-green letters begging to know: IS YOURS A KOOL LOVE? For two years he had watched girls in the hall writhe when a certain boy passed, rolling their eyeballs and pretending to collapse onto the friends giggling beside them; for two years he had watched as most of the other boys in his class drifted uneasily into some kind of sober association with this or that girl. None of these things had called forth a recognition.

His biggest surprise was the music. For years Asa had listened to music for an hour or so every night as he lay in the dark in bed. His transistor radio fit neatly under the curve of his hip beneath the covers, and the pink wire of an earphone snaked invisibly up his side. Several times Dave or his mother had popped into his room while the radio was playing its hidden tunes, and neither had ever detected a thing. He was completely secure. Snug in the dark, lying on his back, he absorbed the songs that came to him through the night. They sank right into his bones. Somehow his mind and body joined up to know these tunes, better than he knew anything. After a while "This Magic Moment" and "Our Day Will Come" and "What's Your Name" and "It's Too Late" and fifty others seemed no longer to come *to* him up the pink wire, but rather to come *from* him, as if he had only to open his mouth and create them, full blown, in all their sonic blare and nuance.

And what, exactly, did he know from this music? When Chuck Willis's voice throated upward on each stretched syllable of the phrase "she's gone" (wailing the two words into nine distinct sounds at one point), when The Drifters dropped into the mysterious swing of the refrain "sweeter than wine . . . softer than a summer night," when the distant voices (the Romantics?) sighed with a kind of merry resignation behind Ruby as she promised "and we'll have everything"—what did this teach him?

For two years it taught him nothing he could spell out. Then one night he lay in the dark listening to Timi Yuro say that the love of a boy could change a girl into a woman—and it hit him. The words, all of them he had ever heard, in every song—they were words of love. They were about—or were supposed to be about—his feelings for Jean. Or, perhaps, it was this way: his feelings for Jean were supposed to be what these songs described.

Chuck Willis had felt what Asa felt? And *sung* about it? And The Drifters—all that your-lips-touching-mine business—was that supposed to be happening? Was that what he should be wanting? For the next few days he shuddered every time another explicit lyric careened into his awareness; where before he could snap his fingers and cut a quick step while singing "These arms of mine . . ." he now thought of the actual arms, and what wasn't between them, and how much they would not know what to do if something were—and then he forced himself to think about something else.

The pressure began to squeeze. He couldn't run away, but he couldn't figure everything out by himself. He faced the fact that he needed some help; he needed to talk to somebody. Somebody who had brought love out of the silence, and put it to work. Somebody who had made love the decisive thing.

T W O

SINCE HER LAST STAY IN THE HOSPITAL, ASA'S MOTHER'S life had changed. She came home just before the sixth grade started, and·she was very settled. Not depressed: she smiled a great deal, with good humor and all that, but she sat a lot and watched things. Before, most of the time she had been wild with energy, constantly active, sometimes scary, always interesting. When he got home from school, she might be composing a symphonic mystery meal using ten pots and twelve mixing bowls, flour and goo all over the kitchen, a meal that never appeared on the dinner table; she might be on a ladder painting some of the shutters yellow, quitting halfway through and leaving Dave to mutter and Asa to scrape paint for three weekends. Sometimes, too, the whole house was heavy with a day's worth of darkness, and his mother was asleep. But even the sleep days were extreme enough to be intriguing, in the whole mix of things.

But for the past year when Asa got home from school every day, his mother was watching old movies on television in the living room. She greeted him cheerily from the sofa, reaching up to pull him down for a kiss. At least one window was always open and the air was pretty fresh, but the blinds were down. She said one or the other of her pills made her eyes sensitive.

Asa always sat with her for a few minutes in front of the television set, answering her questions about school. She almost never looked at the screen while he was there. She held his hand and asked him about his day. He, on the other hand, found himself watching. If something happened on the screen, he would interrupt his own school report to point it out to her; he did not want her to miss anything on his account. She never even glanced, but continued to regard him with an expectant smile.

Every day, after fifteen minutes, he got up and

went to his room and got her pills. She always had water in the living room, but he brought her an extra glassful anyway. She gulped the pills down with her eyes on the screen; but watching her eyes, he could tell she wasn't paying attention to the movie at those moments. She was pretending to watch, pretending the pills were nothing, not even a distraction, but in her eyes he saw a flare of terror and disgust as sharp as a struck match. He left her alone for a while then, coming back through the room a few times just to check up silently.

But today he did not leave. She swallowed her pills, settled back with the brief rage in her eyes, and stared at the screen. After a few minutes she looked at him, puzzled.

"What is it?" she said.

"I want to ask you about something." Once again, he did not meet her gaze. On the screen, a young man whose hair was shiny with pomade stared sadly out the window of an elegant apartment at the lights of a city far below. From the slick hair, the rich material of the curtains, and the way he smoked his cigarette, Asa could tell the movie was from the 1930s. The way they filmed cigarettes in the thirties was different: the smoke looked like rich perfume made visible. A closeup showed the man's eyes gazing out through a swirling haze that would have gagged Asa. But this guy took in a breath and let out a sigh: he had bigger things on his mind than air. Asa coughed.

"What do you want to ask about?" said his mother. She was watching the screen now too.

Asa said, "What do you do when you are in love?"

He had expected her to laugh or something like that. But she spoke very easily, without effort. She said, "Well, you enjoy the way you feel."

He waited a respectful moment, then pressed. "Yes, but what do you—you know—*do*? I mean— if you feel all of a sudden you have to *do* something?"

She looked at him. "Well, most people *talk*." She said it as if she didn't think all that highly of talking, or perhaps of doing what most people did. They both looked back at the television. Now there were shots of a young woman with lipstick that looked black buying something in a department store. It was a watch, a man's watch, rectangular and large. The young woman wore a flat, dense little hat that looked like a round book.

Asa said, "I suppose you've got to talk before you do anything else."

His mother was silent for a moment. The young woman on TV was certainly talking, telling the clerk wrapping her watch about what a wonderful fellow she was purchasing it for. She sounded nervous, as if she were auditioning for the role in the movie. Asa's mother said, "You don't necessarily *have* to talk. There are other ways to communicate."

"Like what? What—" he hesitated only an instant—"what do *you* do when you're in love?"

She smiled. "Well," she said, "I've always found it very natural to leave town." Then she laughed, hard enough to make her cough. One of the pills always made her very dry. Asa handed her one of her water glasses, and she drank. Then she took Asa's hand and looked at him.

He met her eyes. "Why do I want to do this at all?" he said. "For a long time it's been enough just to feel things. Now all of a sudden I want to get it out. Why is that?"

"You want to share something you've made. Just like with the comic books you wrote and drew in the fifth grade. You put all this work into making something, and naturally you want to show it off. It's human nature."

"I'm not sure I 'made' this."

"Oh, yes, you did. It did not just happen to you. It never does. We like to think that sometimes." Her gaze did not falter, but for an instant something jerked in her eyes. She went on. "When we love someone it is because we built that feeling, bit by bit. It's a *choice*. It's what we make only for ourselves, like me baking three cakes and eating them all while you and Dave were away for the Duke-Carolina game that weekend."

He looked away, then back. "Even," he said, "even love in the family? Even that—you choose that?"

She thought for a long moment. "No," she said. "It's different. Mothers, kids, fathers—you don't have to choose that. But you do have to make it. You make it, you build it."

"Bit," he said, "by bit."

She stared at him. He wondered how they had

gotten onto this; here he had started with talk about his feelings for Jean, but in ten minutes he had pulled his mom to the edge of someplace he probably did not want to take her. But she looked away briefly, the moment passed, and she brought herself back to his questions. "There's another reason you're feeling this," she said, with a smile so soft it looked wistful. "You just want to make the girl you love happy."

He frowned. "Happy?" On the TV the man with the pomade was sitting at a table in a restaurant. Smoke from a cigarette in his hand curled around his head like a turban; he looked impatient as a spoiled sultan as he asked a waiter what the time was.

His mother tapped his knee with one finger. "Yes, sweetheart. Happy. Look at me." He did. She put the one finger under his chin, very gently. "When a girl knows a boy loves her, that—more than anything that can happen to her, until she has a child—gives her happiness."

"What if she doesn't love him?"

"It has nothing to do with her feelings for him. It's a gift, that's all. And when you get a gift, you feel good. Doesn't matter if you haven't got a gift ready to give in return. Something as fine as love from someone as nice as you—well, knowing about it means a lot. It can mean *everything*."

There was noise from the screen. They both looked. The young woman was squealing and gasping with her eyes closed, her chin on the dark-wool shoulder of the pomaded man and her hands white on his dark-wool back. His neck was bent forward, but stiff. The light pinged off his hair; the woman was wearing another strange little hat. Asa pointed and said, "Is that it?"

"Who knows?" his mother said. "You can never tell by looking."

They stared as the movie ended with a swell of music. Words rolled by on the screen. Asa looked at his watch. "Be right back," he said.

He went upstairs to his room and took another pill from another bottle in his bureau. When he brought it back to his mother, she took it in her hand but did not put it in her mouth right away. "Sit down, honey," she said. She looked serious.

"Take your pill," he said.

"Sit down."

He sat down. She put the pill in her mouth. He handed her a glass of water, and she sipped and swallowed. "Asa," she said. "Tell me what this love you feel *does*, for *you*. The biggest thing it does. The best thing."

He thought. She waited. He saw she was on the edge of something again, waiting for his answer. He couldn't figure out what she might be hoping for or fearing, so he told the truth. "It makes me feel good about everything. Even things in my life that don't have anything to do with—with her. It—it's just something that's always there to feel good about."

His mother closed her eyes and smiled. "Yes," she said. "That's it."

"Okay," he said, suddenly flushed.

She looked toward the window. Holding her hand out toward him, she opened it and revealed the pill, a white capsule on her shadowed skin.

"Hey," he said. "Mom."

"Feeling good *about* something—about *everything*," she said, still looking the other way. "Whereas this"—she rolled the pill a little on her palm—"this makes you feel *good*, but about *nothing*. That's what it's for. That's—whew. Where I am, apparently." She grunted a chuckle and looked at him. "That's where I have to start, I guess. But you know what?" She put her hands together and shook them, then made two fists and held them out to him. "You know what, Asa?"

He stared at her, refusing to look at her hands. He tried to appear stern. "You should take that. It's my responsibility."

"Here's what," she said. Her eyes were bright. "I think it's been long enough feeling this phony sweetness. Asa—" She opened both of her hands, and he looked despite his resolve; both were empty. She put them on his wrists and squeezed. "Listen—I've got it, too. I've got enough inside to make me feel good *about* things." She patted his arms. "You've been a good young man, taking charge of my pills, taking such good care of me. And *I've* been good. I've taken every pill except once, when Dave and I were going to dinner and I didn't want to feel dopey, but we had a fight so I took them later. God, it's been, what, a year, more. You've been perfect. But the treatment's over."

"I want you to be okay," Asa said. "I don't want

you to have trouble."

She shook his arms. "Trouble," she said, "doesn't just come from feeling bad when things are going fine. Trouble can also come from feeling good when you shouldn't. Hey, listen." She put her hands up to his face and smiled as deeply as he could remember seeing in recent years. "There's nothing to be afraid of. Things happen; they don't stop. Look what's happened to you while I've been sitting here taking feelgood pills and watching TV. You've gone and fallen in love and gotten to be man enough to want to do something with it." She held her hands up. "Probably just as much has happened to me, but I would never know it, not while I keep sitting here smiling at nothing."

Asa could not help asking, "What could have happened? To you."

She held his eyes, still smiling. "Well," she said, "I could be in love and not even know it." They watched each other carefully. Then, only a little more softly, she added: "Or not in love, Asa. And I wouldn't know that either."

He swallowed. His throat was dry. She handed

him her water, and he sipped. "Okay," he said. "I'll go along. I won't tell. About not taking the pills."

"Then I won't tell," she said, "about the love."

"Mine?" he asked. "Or yours?"

She laughed. "Yours is your business," she said. "Mine—" She shook her head, and he saw the match strike behind her eyes again. "Mine *should* be only my business, too. But—God help us, Asa—it never ends up that way, does it?"

She looked at him. He looked at the TV. Another movie was starting.

THREE

IT TOOK HIM ONLY A WEEK. HE DID NOT FORCE THINGS by trying to get Jean off by herself somewhere; he waited until it happened naturally, as if the movements of the class were some kind of tide and it was best to let the tide run its course.

One Tuesday he went in early from recess so that he could take a biography of Mickey Mantle back to the library and renew it. He walked into the classroom, and there she was, sitting at her desk, reading. They were alone.

She looked up, and watched him approach. He stood beside her desk. Holding her finger in her place, she closed the book. Her desk was in the row nearest the windows; the thin brightness of autumn was shiny around her. She smiled, waiting for whatever it was.

He had not planned anything. He had hoped the moment would come and he would know what to do. He had hoped it would be simple. It was.

"I love you, Jean," he said.

That was all. His heart was steady; his breath was deep. He waited for a moment, politely, to see if she wanted to respond. When he saw her cheeks flood with color and her eyes widen with something that looked like fear, he made a little bow and withdrew, taking a moment to get the book from his desk. She did not speak, and he did not look back.

On the way to the library, he felt for the first time the uncanny strength he held in his body: his legs could launch a leap to the corridor ceiling should he choose not to restrain their power in these small strides, and his eyes, if he really opened them, could beam great light upon things, enriching colors, revealing facts. He looked at the book in his hands. Probably he could squeeze it back into wood pulp.

Jean's expression had puzzled him for a moment, because he plainly saw that it was fear. She had been afraid. Why? He started to work on this, and in a few moments found the answer: *She thinks she is still a child.* He smiled. That was it; that was what she thought. Her childhood—*that* was what she had seen, all of a sudden, from the other side, from her future. He knew, because he had just taken the same step himself. He smiled again. Well, there was time. He would be here, waiting as long as it took. He would be here when Jean began to grow comfortable becoming herself.

He ran home from school and arrived with his full wind. On the way up the steps of his house he considered taking a deep breath and blowing the door off its hinges; he actually saw it toppling through the foyer. He chose to open it quietly instead. Then, stepping in, he smelled Dave's after-shave. He stopped. And he knew. It came to him in a heartbeat why Dave was home at such a weird time of the day. Asa allowed himself a quick, quiet sigh, then rubbed his eyes, stood up straight, got ready. By the time his mother's voice came from the living room, asking him to come in, he was all set.

He entered the room and glanced at them, sitting in the two chairs, facing the sofa. He saw only shapes. The lights were out, the blinds were down, the curtains were closed, the windows were shut, and the television was off. He dropped onto the sofa like a leaf falling into a dark pool somewhere in a forest.

"Asa," said his mother. Yes. Amazing: here it came. He almost smiled at the familiarity of it. He wanted to tell her she could stop speaking right there. But he let her go on, and the words sounded again: decision, difficult, respect, no love, divorce, best for all, moving away. He was surprised how well he remembered them, and how nearly they were repeated. There were some differences, of course: he and his mother were not leaving immediately with one suitcase, but tomorrow at noon; they were going not to the beach, but to an apartment Dave had kindly found for them in Raleigh; in fact, Dave—no end to his kindness—was driving them there, in what she clearly called *his* car.

Another difference this time, of course, was that the man they were leaving was sitting right there, lumpy and still in the dark, listening, presumed to agree, ready to be helpful in delivering them out of his life. Asa looked at Dave and knew with a warm certainty that he and Dave, in silence, were feeling at least one thing the same: surely they were both relieved. There was more, of course— he knew that Dave, as a husband, as a boyfriend from olden times, was possessed by a mess of other feelings. But merely as a stepfather, surely Dave felt relieved, even blessed. Again Asa nearly smiled, tenderly, at the fact that here, at the end of their time together, they had a lot in common: the yearning for freedom from each other.

Asa's mother finished talking. This time she did not chatter and fret. She spoke with a commanding confidence, in a tone Asa had never heard before. He did not trust it entirely—he had been duped by her chipper bravado before—but at least she seemed to be taking wing this time with a certain forcefulness, and surely that was preferable to wincing and stumbling. In the darkness Asa saw her turn her head pertly toward Dave: it was his turn to say a few words now, if he liked.

Dave cleared his throat. Asa waited, silently sending Dave a message: *You don't have to make a speech*. Dave evidently got the message. After an awkward pause, all he said was, "Sorry, Sport." Asa stood up and said, "Me too. I'd better go pack."

So he did. It took longer than he expected. He had to admit he had gotten soft: living in this house for nearly three years had taken the snap out of his reflexes. Once, a few years ago, it had seemed he was packing every other month, and he had refined packing to a crisp drill. Now he started slowly, holding things he had acquired in this place and savoring them a little before putting them into boxes. He reflected on the view from the windows, the light in the room, the smell of mothballs and cedar in the closet. Then he snapped out of it. His old drive returned with a rush of efficiency: the point was to pack, to get ready, to move. It was, to tell the truth, kind of exciting. Moving—what was wrong with it, as a word, as a concept? As a life? Everything had to move; you could not really grow without movement. Pity the people who had to stay stuck in one place. Put it in a box and take to the road.

He finished just after dark. His mother looked in once, to bring him a plate of cold fried chicken and potato salad, while he was finishing with his comic-book collection. She said nothing, just left the plate and blew a kiss he did not look up to receive, nodding an acknowledgment instead: he was a busy guy. They both knew how this whole thing worked; they had shared it before, they were partners, really. His heart swelled with the closeness of it, this partnership, this resumption of the familiar adventure. He had a sense of orderliness now—a conviction that it was good to live the life you had established, especially if you had established it with someone. As he ate, hastily tearing the chicken, he was surrounded by the special bliss that came when someone gave him something. A sense of opportunity came, too—for strength, and no-nonsense action, and perhaps, pride. He was a boy who appreciated an opportunity to be strong, so a wave of gratitude followed his bliss.

He went downstairs when he had finished. The public parts of the house looked much the same; he knew the furniture and stuff would be packed by movers. His mother was finishing in her bedroom. Dave was nowhere to be seen. Perhaps he was spending the night in a motel or something. That would be decorous of him. Asa went out through the screened porch, into the backyard, for a last look at the moonlight on the sycamore that grew in the middle. But as soon as he stepped onto the grass he smelled Dave's after-shave again, and heard himself called by name from the darkness.

He walked out toward the tree. There was no moon. In what would have been the tree's shadow, Dave lay on a long beach chair. He seemed to be doing nothing. Asa realized that in fact he had nothing to do: everyone else was busy packing. He was staying out of their way. No doubt he would be moving, too; but for the moment the act of leaving belonged to Asa and his mother.

Dave moved on the chair. "Sit down with me," he said. His voice was not soft so much as watery. He did not sound like himself. He sounded injured. Asa, who was feeling so bouncy, wondered if they had so much in common right now after all—or if his own bounciness was all that true. He sat down, and Dave hugged him close.

Asa let himself be hugged; he even tried to lean into it a little. There had been a time, in the first couple of years after Dave and his mother had married, when Asa had wished for the kind of comfortable, casual-hugging relationship he saw other boys have with their dads. He believed he had enjoyed such a relationship with his true father, but he couldn't really remember. It was surprising that he couldn't remember, really: he could remember almost everything in his life. Things about himself and his father, back in the days before he knew such things as divorce were possible had been wiped out, as if some hip skepticism looked on his innocence with scorn and obliterated its traces.

Despite his hope, however, he and Dave could never quite get the hang of being offhand. It was not possible for one to touch the other, or say even a few words, with true ease. Everything meant something, to both of them. They were watchful, taut. No hugs.

But now Asa settled in with his back against Dave's chest, and they sat looking up into the black sky showing through the tree limbs. The sycamore smelled like brown sugar. Dave said, "I don't know if you know this, but I want you to: I love you."

"Oh," said Asa.

Dave sighed. "I don't blame you. I wouldn't believe it either. But it's true. It's true in spite of how hard I *tried* to love you."

Asa frowned. "What?"

Dave shifted a little in the chair, sighed. "Well, see, that was the problem, for a long time. Trying, I mean. See—I knew I *had* to. I had to love you. It was . . . necessary. I was marrying your mother, and that meant I was taking you, too. So I just tried like heck. But I'm no good at that, Sport—I hate almost anything I have to try to do. I hate *hav-*

ing to do anything." He waited a moment. "I bet you can understand that part."

"Yes," said Asa.

"Right. You don't like having to do something either. We're alike in that way. We're alike a lot of ways, really. That's one reason we don't get along better."

"Maybe so," said Asa.

Dave chuckled. "You don't sound like you believe it."

Asa said, "I guess I see some ways we get at each other because we are both guys. There's *that*. But I guess I don't ever feel like we're the same *kind* of guys."

Dave thought about it for a while. He laughed a watery laugh. "I guess you're right." He sighed, and hugged Asa closer.

Asa sat for a while, being hugged. He *could* leave it at that. He *could* sit quietly and in another twenty hours this guy would be out of his life. Certainly a year ago he could have exercised a strategic restraint, he could have skipped the last, few fine points. But something had changed. He said, "You don't know who I am."

Dave said nothing. Asa went on. "You know who you'd like me to be, and I think that's the kid you love."

He felt Dave tense a little, harden up in the chest, and start to speak. But then Dave relaxed again, and said only: "I guess I should say I'm sorry."

Asa smiled at the clever phrase. "*Are* you sorry, then?" he pressed.

Dave struggled for a moment, then gave in. "No," he said, forcefully. "No, by God, I'm not."

"Ah," said Asa.

"Because," said Dave, warming up, "because maybe who I want you to be is better than who you are. And I'll tell you one thing for sure—you can bet I only want it to *help* you, help you be a better person, have a better life."

"Even if it's someone else's life."

Dave laughed, shallow and bitter. "Fine, son. All righty. You go ahead and enjoy your own precious self and your own precious life. Have a ball. To me, though, the prospects don't look all that hot. I hoped maybe you learned some things. You're in for some surprises, see; the world isn't just sitting out there waiting for Asa to be who he is in all his glory, so it can bestow its blessing. You have to meet the world halfway."

Asa waited a moment, then said, "Halfway doesn't sound bad."

Dave snapped, "What do you mean by that?"

Asa sighed. He was tired. "Just what I said. Halfway would be fine. You always came *more* than halfway. You came right up into my face. No room left. But never mind. I'm cold. I'm going in. I'm sorry about you and Mom. I know it's been hard having me along, stuck into the whole thing. I'm sorry you had to try to love me and it didn't work."

"But I told you," said Dave with a kind of pleading, as Asa stood up. "I told you: I do love you, Asa. I don't know *why*. There's a lot of reasons I shouldn't on the face of it."

Asa laughed. "Thanks a lot."

Dave ignored him. "But you've got to believe me, son. And I'll miss you. I know I'm going to miss you. Bad."

Asa faced him. In the darkness he could just see the outline of Dave's head, the pale motion of his mouth. He looked at the man. It was incredible that this indistinct thing had been the source of so many excruciatingly exact requirements in his life. He sighed again, and shivered. Time to go.

"Well," he said, "good night."

"Good night, Asa." Dave's voice was watery again. Almost in a whisper, he added: "I love you."

Asa started to go, then hesitated. He looked at the dark outline. Politely, gently, with all the cheery-but-sober charm he could muster, he said, "Then I'd *like* to say: I love you too."

He turned away. But it wasn't enough. From the chair Dave called for the certainty of clarification: "You do, Asa? Do you?"

Asa stopped. He heard the pleading. It was almost soft. It was almost openhearted. It was almost, almost halfway.

One more time, Dave asked: "Then you do, Asa? You love me?"

Standing still in the dark, Asa said nothing. What was he waiting for? Why not just snap the obvious answer at Dave and leave him in pain? After all, Asa knew the answer, did he not? Well—

that was where the hesitation took hold. Asa realized with a shiver that suddenly he was *not* so certain; it was not so easy after all to say "No." The question hung in the dark air, *Do you love me, too?* and for the first time in his life Asa did not want to know an answer. If the heart could betray one's good sense—if love could take such liberties as to fasten onto stepfathers—then what hope was there for a boy of intelligence and will? What justice? Asa did not want to know. He stood there with his eyes closed, trying to feel absolutely nothing, holding his breath in the hope that enlightenment, for once, would pass him by. Then, quietly, without a word, he began to walk back toward the house.

FOUR

THE MORNING AT SCHOOL GOT AWAY FROM HIM. Withdrawing required a lot of little official duties. He looked for Jean before homeroom, but she wasn't with her usual friends on the grounds. She came into homeroom at the last minute, just before roll call; then Asa was called out, to go down to the office. He wanted to tell her himself, that he was moving away. He wanted to tell her things did not change because of this. He hoped this was actually true, in some wild way he couldn't imagine. He wanted to say it, anyhow.

Then, before first period, Jean's friend Brenda rushed up to him outside the classroom doorway. She looked at him quickly as if he were something between a hero and a ferocious animal, and she pressed a balled-up paper napkin into his hand. "From Jean," she said. "She *means* it."

Carrying the napkin, he took his seat, and stared over at Jean. She was looking down into her lap, at nothing.

In the middle of class he was called down to the office again; as he left he zipped a glance at Jean. She wasn't even watching him. In the hall, he stopped and unwadded the napkin.

Inside were two small candy hearts, one pale purple, the other white. They were the kind kids gave out at Valentine's Day, with pink letters printed on them; his heart sank as he remembered such messages as "Squeeze me!" and "Cute Guy!" Maybe she *was* still a kid. That would make leaving a little easier, perhaps.

But then he straightened the hearts out on his palm and read them. On each of them, the letters said: *I love you.* Twice: *I love you. I love you.* Two. In other words, *I love you, too.* He read them again. It was a smart bit of wordplay. He believed the smartness, and the hearts. He believed Jean. Okay: she loved him, too. He straightened himself. His feelings balled up and dropped, right through the bottoms of his feet.

He went to the office and signed whatever he had to sign, then came back to class. He nodded at Mrs. Halterman at the blackboard and made his way to his seat. He did not look at Jean, but he could see that her face was turned toward him. It stayed that way, throughout the class: her head was erect and her face shone at him like a spotlight. He could see it. He could feel it. Her attention pulled at him like a great, calm tide.

It was clear: she knew now that he had read the hearts. She had hidden from him that morning like a child, until her message was delivered.

Now, with her new power, she demanded that he meet her feelings, face to face. It was just the way he had felt when he told her he loved her. It was her turn now.

With five minutes left in class, he could not resist. He looked over at her.

She was waiting for him. Her face was clear— no hope or fear or adoration or humor. It was a naked face. It looked as if it had never been bared to the world before. Now it was bared only to him. Her eyes were bright and fixed, and at a glance someone might have said they looked almost fierce, hungry. But they were not fierce; they were not hungry. They simply looked at what was outside—Asa—and showed what was inside—Jean. Showed, and *gave*: in her open, naked, brilliant gaze, Jean was giving herself to him, child, girl, and woman.

He could not look away. He had no idea what his face showed—fear, like hers yesterday? Grief? A giving of his own?—because he had no idea what he was feeling. Things whirled before him, demanding consideration. There was Jean, right here; there was a call of mystery from the life he would start tomorrow, somewhere else, a life in which the spirit of adventure was ready to clear the heart of longings best left behind; there was his mother, spiraling close and familiar, spiraling strange and away.

He was certain of only one thing: He knew he would always *move*, inside and out. But Jean's face, more than anything, was still. It offered itself in silence and stillness: to explore, to accept what was being given, one would have to join the silence, find the stillness, stop moving. He knew: his moving would never stop. And he knew, somehow, that this showed.

In case it didn't, Mrs. Halterman stopped the lesson a minute before the bell and began to speak. He heard his name. Without looking away, he listened; he could see Jean do the same. "We are very sorry," Mrs. Halterman was saying, "that we are losing Asa. Today is his last day in our school, and we want to wish him luck and tell him that we will miss him."

Other faces turned his way, and a ripple of sound passed quickly over the class: disappointment, then curiosity. Asa had to look away from

Jean to glance around, smile, nod. The bell rang. With a few more looks at him and a couple of waves, the kids left. That was it. One day he had stood outside their classroom door waiting to get in, and they had let him in. He *had* been completely in there for these years, hadn't he? It really *was* the inside, wasn't it? But now things had turned inside out again. He was to go. Good-bye, Ace, have a nice life.

He heard a sound from Jean's direction and turned. She was up, Brenda was glaring at him, together they were rushing out, Brenda's arm around the smaller girl's shoulders, which were down, sunk, moving. Brenda was hating him hard with her eyes; he could barely look past them to Jean, but he got a glimpse of her face, and with a shock he saw there was no sadness there. There was only fury. She shook with it; the tears that caught the overhead light on her cheeks were tears of rage. He rose in his desk, tried to say something, but Brenda had her out the door. He stayed halfway up, awkward, staring after them. The room was empty. Nobody came back. Furious! The heat of it prickled his face like sunburn. Well, what did he expect? Sadness, probably, was for kids.

FIVE

ON THE WAY OUT OF TOWN THEY HAD A FLAT TIRE. ASA helped Dave jack the car up, and he took the lug nuts Dave handed him and placed them in the hubcap of the afflicted wheel. But when they had secured the spare and jacked the car down, they discovered that the spare was flat too. Dave cursed. Asa volunteered to hitchhike to a service station they had passed a couple of miles back. Strangely enough, he was allowed to do this. The first car that came along stopped for him. In it were three people, two men and a woman, who hastily and urgently asked him about his religion while spitting politely into Dixie cups every sentence or so. He said he loved Jesus just fine, and asked them why they spit so much. They told him they "took snuff," adding that it was godlier than smoking cigarettes. At the filling station he thanked them and got out.

He waited in the station while the tow truck went and fetched Dave and his mother and the car. The three of them waited for a while, to find out that a tire would have to be ordered from a station across town; the car would not be ready for another two hours. Asa, drinking Dr Pepper and studying random maps of the U.S. pulled from a dispenser, was content. But his mother and Dave seemed restless, and began to exchange odd looks.

"You know—" said his mom.

"Yeah—"said Dave.

"It's already so late—"

"Wasting time—"

"So close to home—"

"Movers aren't coming 'til tomorrow afternoon—"

"Make better time—"

"The boy's exhausted—"

Asa watched this dialogue pass between them, looking up from the highways of Colorado. He could see them collaborating on an idea, showing more and more with each comment that they thought the same thing; he could see, too, that they both knew the idea was bogus. But safe, somehow: in the artificiality of this sudden free time, seemingly forced upon them, they could trick themselves and not get into trouble.

They decided, face to face, with a last long look. Then Dave went to ask the station owner to run them back to town, and Asa's mother came over to him. He looked up. Her eyes were gleaming.

"Honey," she said. "Guess what! We're going home, for one more night."

They piled into an old Mercury that sagged badly to the passenger side. Asa rode in front. On the seat between him and the driver was a fuel pump; at his feet were two parts of a clutch assembly. As soon as they arrived home, Dave and his mother went out into the yard to sit on the long beach chair together. Asa watched them sit, then went to the telephone.

He had memorized Jean's number long before, not because he had ever come close to calling her, but merely because it was one more thing about her that could be committed to the sum inside him. As he dialed, he realized he had designed a speech in the back of his mind while he looked over those maps. He was ready for her anger, ready to rediscover his strength, to rely on the undeniable goodness of his feelings. Nothing could go wrong if he stuck to them, if he stuck to love.

She answered. He hesitated: her voice sounded quite chirpy. This was not what he had expected, but he spoke anyway: "Jean. This is Asa."

She said, "Oh! Hi!" He filtered every iota of the two syllables through his finest scrutiny, but he could not find the slightest tone of anger, regret, frustration. There was only good cheer, nice and shallow, open and free.

"I wanted to talk about today," he began.

She laughed. "What a crazy day!" she said. Something about the way she said it—something about that *crazy*—warned him off. With a shiver he knew she wasn't referring to his part of the day, but to something that had happened later, after he left. He forced himself to remember that he had left halfway. Hey, there was a whole afternoon remaining, for crazy stuff to happen!

She seemed eager to talk, so he simply said, "Oh, yes?"

"Well," she said, laughing again, "it was pretty weird. I certainly never expected it—I mean, I wasn't even paying attention much or anything. But—well, do you know Robert Pontiac?" He did, slightly; Robert Pontiac was the only kid in school as small as Asa, and nearly as shrewd. Somehow Robert capitalized on his smallness in a way that made him cute to the girls and appealingly funky to the boys. He could talk dirty with a certain daring that passed for funniness, he got C's and D's, he had the perfect careless walk; he carried off much more of a rough-and-tumble swagger than could be expected from a runt. His older brothers were famous athletes in the school's history. His nickname, an honor strictly among the boys, was Booger. Asa said, "Yes, I know Robert."

"Well—" And off Jean went in a narrative romp. It seemed she was eating her lunch, and a friend of Robert's called Brenda over, and then the friend took Brenda to where Robert was sitting, and then Brenda came back, alone, and sat down breathless. And then, amazing as it was, Brenda told her that Robert liked her.

"Can you imagine that?" Jean said, with an incredulous laugh.

"Can I imagine liking you?" Asa said, incredulous in his turn. But she breezed on: Robert Pontiac! What in the world did he like about *her*? She knew he was a pretty bad student, and he hung around with all those athlete types. Whereas she— she was just this brainy type, always buried in a book. How in the world had he come upon *her*?

Asa knew, of course. He knew what had been released from Jean in all its radiance, and how the wind picked it up and spread it like light and scent and sound. *He* had not taken it in, so out it went, and Robert Pontiac was just the sort of keenly alert weasel to snatch the signs from the air and zero in.

But Asa said nothing. The funny thing was— Jean was really *asking*. She really didn't *know*. He could tell she wasn't even sure *he* did, either, but just in case, she was checking. And certainly he *could* explain. He almost did, too, with a resigned goodwill, out of habit. But it was too much to ask; he flared at the cruelty of her lightness, her fleet forgetting. Then he thought: who was *he* to get angry? What rights remained that he had not refused? So he said nothing; he let her run on with her query until she trailed off. Then it was obvious to both of them that the conversation was over.

"Well," she said, "guess I've got to go."

"Sure," he said. "Me too." But he could not just drop away. Some sense of honor compelled him to a last task: to acknowledge with gratitude, at least, the first declaration of love he had ever received from a woman. Whatever hopes he had tricked up for this phone call had been foolish. He had to accept that. But before he moved on, a grace was called for.

"Jean," he said, sounding formal even to himself, but so what? This was, after all, a kind of formality: "Jean, I just want you to know—that the hearts will always mean everything to me."

And an instant after speaking, he knew with a pierce of insight exactly what Jean was going to say. It gave him an extra heartbeat to get ready— to understand that grace is given, not always received; to clench his honor closed before her words slipped in and undid it. He moved, gently but quickly, to hang up the phone, just as she asked, with all the simplicity of a memory wiped clean by new ardor, "What hearts?"

A moment later, sitting in the darkening living

room, he felt better. Why not? He had the hearts, after all; he had the words, *I love you I love you*, printed clean. He had gotten them in what was suddenly his past, but they needn't stay there. He pulled out the candies. In the twilight he could just read them, pale on his palm. *I love you I love you*. He had the *words*. There was a good thing about words: they could rise away from circumstances, they could take their meaning with them, they could move right along with you. And if a fellow had *these* words, these above all, then surely, something was in store in the future. Somewhere down the road, surely, these words would be made good.